I0542701

THE SPIDER:
KING OF THE RED KILLERS

MASTER OF **MEN** !

THE SPIDER®

KING OF
THE RED KILLERS

By Grant Stockbridge

STEEGER BOOKS • 2020

© 1935, 2020 Argosy Communications, Inc. All rights reserved.

THE SPIDER® is a trademark of Argosy Communications, Inc.
Authorized and produced under license.

PUBLISHING HISTORY

"King of the Red Killers" originally appeared in the September, 1935 (Vol. 6, No. 4) issue of *The Spider* magazine. Copyright 2020 by Argosy Communications, Inc. All rights reserved.

ALL RIGHTS RESERVED

No part of this book may be reproduced or utilized in any form or by any means, electronic or mechanical, without permission in writing from the publisher.

This edition has been marked via subtle changes, so anyone who reprints from this collection is committing a violation of copyright.

Visit STEEGERBOOKS FOR more books like this.

CHAPTER 1
THE SPIDER'S WARNING

THE ELEVATOR operator's cap was dragged down over his right eyebrow. He leaned against the gate with a cigarette dangling from his lips. "Listen, babe," he said flatly, "you ain't goin' up to de boss wit' no phony stories about de Spider comin' here. De boss...."

The man's voice choked off as the girl's hand flew from her waist and presented the point of a slim, long knife to his belly.

"Up, fool," she ordered softly.

The cigarette dropped from the man's lips. He went backwards into the elevator before the pressure of the knife and the door slammed shut. When it had begun its upward moan, the shadows moved in the stairway just to the right of the shaft. From the blackness a man stepped forward on alert, silent feet. His shoulders were twisted as if by the painful giant hands of disease, so that he walked hunched far forward. A black, slouch hat was on his head and he wore a long black cape that accentuated, rather than masked, his affliction.

Standing before the elevator door, the man stopped. Light slanting under the wide brim of his hat showed a mouth that was a straight, lipless line.

"So," he chuckled softly, "he thinks the presence of the Spider a phony story?"

The mouth twisted into a slow, tight smile that was strangely

sinister. No one seeing this man could have mistaken his identity. And if that one had guilt upon his conscience—the blood
of a fellow being, the rifling of a poor man's till—he would have
fled in screaming terror. For the Spider was known throughout
the length and breadth of the land as the avenger of the innocent, a lone wolf of justice who struck down the guilty without
mercy!

He lifted the Spider's head high
in the air before El Gaucho!

The hunchback turned toward the stairway and once more it was as if the shadows moved. There was no sound as he swiftly mounted the steps. That was well for the Spider. If the criminals gathered here tonight to plot robbery and murder believed him present, they would hunt him down ruthlessly with machine guns. And the Underworlds of the universe would shriek for joy at his death!

But the Spider's progress was noiseless, unfaltering, though the smile faded from his lips. A week ago, he had dared to hope that organized crime was smashed! Now there was bitterness in the gray-blue eyes beneath the hat brim. He had been prosecuting a vigorous war against minor Underworld leaders and killers and they had been fleeing from him with a shrill terror, like frightened rats. No new evil genius had arisen to lead them. Yes, he and Nita van Sloan, the one woman who held his trust and his love, had dared to hope that at last they might claim the happiness they had battled to afford to others. And then this....

In the West, a man calling himself El Gaucho—a queer, mocking name since it meant merely one of the wild-riding cowboys of the South American *pampas*—this butcher of humans had pillaged three towns within three days; the small army of desperados he had gathered about him had swept clean the banks and richer stores, burning homes, and killing wantonly.

In the first raid on Morgantown, Arizona, five men and three women had been shot down on the streets, mercilessly, without other reason than that they had seen the masked faces of the raiders. In Hawleyville, twelve had crumpled before the ruthless guns of the bandits. And in Carson....The Spider felt a cold rage grow within him at the memory of those pitiful reports of last night... a machine gun had sprayed a school yard full of playing children. Twenty-one dead there besides five adults slain in the streets, and the wounded....

IT WAS such insensate criminals as this one who called himself El Gaucho that the Spider had vowed to track down and kill. It mattered not that the man had gathered all the rene-

4

gades from both sides of the Mexican border and schooled them in his murderous assaults. Even though they rallied about him two hundred strong, the Spider would break through to exact the vengeance which the law, somehow, so often failed to get. He had been prepared to fly westward to join battle when he heard a news whisper that struck terror to his heart. Not personal terror. Fear was a thing that the Spider did not know for himself. But terror for the new millions that were threatened.

He had heard that the Underworld, demoralized by the Spider's coldly efficient warfare, was uniting to invite El Gaucho eastward to command them! A united Underworld, working voluntarily under a leader who slaughtered like a Turk! No wonder the Spider had come here tonight! Here it was that the intimidated leaders of the city's robbers, killers, blackmailers and thieves would assemble under the powerful domination of Oscar Piltsdown, whom the liquor racket had known of old. Or so at least the Spider's information hinted. It had been confirmed now by the arrival of the girl to warn Piltsdown. He knew her, too, as it was the business of the Spider to know all the Underworld of importance. She was Yvonne Musette, Piltsdown's latest love.

The Spider was climbing toward the third floor now, hearing the dim murmur of voices from above. Ah, then Yvonne had not yet given the alarm! He had made haste to reach the upper levels before she cried that the Spider was on his way. He must prevent their sending an envoy to El Gaucho. That was the oddest part about the entire menacing business.

A young man named Tom Barker had come to New York

with tales of having seen El Gaucho loot a town, with the boast that he could reach the man again at any time he wished. Police had been seeking Barker to find if he told the truth and the Spider had sought him, too. Tonight he had learned that the Underworld had found Barker first. He had come into the power of Oscar Piltsdown, one of the few remaining leaders of the Underworld whom the Spider had been unable to locate. Unable, that is, until tonight, when he had trailed one of Piltsdown's men to this building which, by daylight, was the gymnasium of an athletic club. And now Piltsdown's current sweetheart, Yvonne Musette, had rushed here to give warning of information obtained, God alone knew where, that the Spider was on his way to call on Piltsdown. The Spider frowned as he circled the elevator shaft and slipped on toward the third floor. He heard voices there....

How had Yvonne learned the Spider's plans? No one but Nita had known his secret and death itself could not have wrested it from her. Still, Yvonne had learned, and the men said to be gathered here with Piltsdown to invite El Gaucho east through the agency of Tom Barker would be warned of the Spider's impending visit....

Once more the grim, hard smile crossed the Spider's lips. Well, even that warning should not save them. He was determined that El Gaucho should not come eastward with an already united Underworld to welcome him. There would be no limit to the man's power, no end to his atrocities, if such an alliance were formed.

Peering from the darkness of the stairway into the hallway of the third floor, the Spider shut speculation from his mind. He could see the girl beside the elevator door, see the elevator operator arguing vehemently with three men who lounged against the wide door opposite. They were careless seeming, those three, but when they moved, their hands were  quick and flexible. Their eyes held a flat, cold gleam. Killers all! If they should see the Spider!

"Cheez," the elevator man was saying, "I'm telling you I couldn't keep her down. She pulls a shiv on me and says she'll gut me if I even open my trap. She did. And damn it to hell, *she meant it!*"

IN THE darkness, the Spider smiled faintly. He thought it very likely Yvonne Musette had meant precisely that. In the Montmartre, whence she came, the *Apache* girls had been known to kill on even less provocation. And there was a certain cold poise about Yvonne....

The girl's small red mouth smiled prettily, "Of course," she agreed, a faint accent clipping her words. "You are one ignoran' peeg. *Attendee, foux!* Listen, fools. I tell you thees Spider is already 'ere. Eeef you do not let me see Oscaire, there will be 'ell to pay!"

The men stirred uneasily, looking at one another. The girl stood straight and still, graceful as a cat with her long, taut body firm beneath the close embrace of her russet-brown dress. The silk caught shimmering highlights from the dim bulb that illuminated the hall. Her face beneath the cloche that pressed down her dark curls was still gently smiling.

One of the men shifted his feet uncertainly, "Listen, Yvonne," he muttered. "The Spider couldn't possibly know about this."

Yvonne shrugged her right shoulder, pursing her red lips. The Spider glanced quickly over the hall and saw that there were only the four men and the girl. Should he allow the girl to get through with her warning, or should he stop her here? If she gave the message, they would be watchful—might even search for him. But also, they would become apprehensive, so that his warning to forget El Gaucho, when he gave it, would carry more force. Furthermore, it was unlikely he could conquer all of them without an alarm being given... Even as he made up his mind, Yvonne acted. She turned as if to enter the waiting elevator, then she darted between the men. Before they could intervene, she had rapped on the door.

The Spider heard her cry: "Oscaire! Oscaire! The Spider comes...."

Then the door slammed shut.

The Spider sprang into instantaneous action. These four men in the hall must be eliminated now, while they were disconcerted by Yvonne's break—while they stared at each other and tried to decide what to do, what was the best time to strike. As the Spider bolted from the darkness of the stairways, his right hand flashed out and his stiffened fingers jabbed at the elevator operator's throat, struck nerve centers which rendered him instantly unconscious.

There was no pause in the Spider's swift movement. His guns

flew to his hands and the two forty-five caliber automatics which he carried in clip holsters beneath his arms struck simultaneously, butt-first, against the napes of two of the guards. Thus far, there had been no sound save the thud of his blows—and the falling operator had not yet reached the floor!

The third guard whirled, with his hand clawing for his gun. Once more the Spider's automatic slashed out, caught the temple. The man collapsed to the floor with a choked cry rising in his throat.

The Spider stood rock-still, guns in hand, before the door through which Yvonne had vanished. Within, he heard the excited gabble of voices and he nodded to himself, smiling thinly. Their own shouting would have drowned the sounds of the swift battle in the hall.

The Spider moved rapidly then, loading the four unconscious men into the elevator cage. He hooked the operator's belt over the handle of the control so that his unconscious weight would start the cage downward as soon as the closing of the door released the safety stop, then slid the gate shut. He turned again toward the door of the room where Piltsdown and Yvonne, and the others who would join with him in the invitation to El Gaucho, were in conference. His lips drew back thinly from his teeth. But the expression was not a smile....

CHAPTER 2
DISASTER THREATENS

A S YVONNE MUSETTE dashed into the room where Piltsdown held conference with twelve other criminals, the men whirled to face her. The room was the main gymnasium of the athletic club and the men had taken careful pains that light should not escape to the street. A long table had been set in the middle of the vast room and the only light came from seven candles in a single, many-branched stick. The shadows in the corners seemed enormous.

"Oscaire! Oscaire!" the girl cried again. "The Spider comes!"

There were thirteen men about the table. They leaped to their feet as one person, and the massive, square-built man who had stood at its head came forward on quick, solid feet to meet the girl. Yvonne seized his arms, pressed close against him.

"For the sake of *le bon Dieu,*" she cried, urgently. "You must leave here at once."

The man patted her shoulder with a thick, short-fingered hand. "Come, come, Yvonne," he rumbled, "the Spider cannot hurt us now."

He turned back toward the head of the table, leading the girl. The other twelve men watched them come, cast apprehensive glances into the dark, looming shadows. The candlelight reached only feebly into the gloom. It gleamed on dangling acrobatic apparatus, on the stanchions of the running track that circled the hall like a balcony, but did not disperse the darkness.

"Listen, Piltsdown," one of the men broke out nervously,

"what's this about the Spider? How do you know he can't hurt us? God! He's killed twenty men in the last month!"

Oscar Piltsdown said nothing until he had regained his seat at the head of the table and pulled the girl down on the arm of his chair. "Pah! It is nothing," he scoffed amiably, blinking mildly at his confreres from behind horn-rimmed spectacles. "Have we not joost planned how to rid ourselves of this fool insect, the Spider? Barker is already started for Newark. Soon he will be flying to see El Gaucho... *Nein*, he cannot harm us. Yvonne joost want to be with her Oscar!"

Yvonne's hands clutched at Piltsdown's shoulder. "No, no!" she said, quickly. "It is true, what I say. I was comin' here to see you, yes. But from my taxi I see a man in a black cape sneak into the alley behin' here. He has the hunchback an'... an' jus' lookin' at heem make me so frighten'!"

Oscar Piltsdown looked up at the girl's dark, comely face with shrewd, blue eyes. The men about the table stirred restively.

"Listen, Piltsdown..." It was the same man who had spoken before, a slenderly built, smooth-haired Latin. "If Yvonne saw the Spider...."

"I did not have a gun," the girl mourned.

"... If Yvonne saw the Spider, we'd better turn on the lights and get the other men...."

Piltsdown grunted. "Pah! We turn on the lights and the police come to see why we are all lighted up at night. They know nothing is supposed to be here. Also we make the Spider's work easier for him. We give him targets... *Pah!* Yvonne is mistake'. And if she is not, then... we *kill* the Spider!"

"Don't be a fool, Piltsdown!"

"I am no fool, *nein.*" Piltsdown shook his heavy head. "This Spider is a man like other men. He can be killed. Meantime, we go on with our plans. Come, my friends, if you work with me, we shall own the city. Yes. Joost that!" He put both his big hands on the table, leaned forward confidentially. His voice lowered: "This Gaucho robs whole cities and nobody can stop him. If someone gets in his way… Poof! He is dead. If Gaucho wish, this Spider is dead, too. Look what Gaucho did tonight."

Piltsdown shook a newspaper at the others about the table. Heavy black headlines across the front pages were smeary with ink.

"Two million dollars!" Piltsdown shouted. "Two million dollars he took tonight. Two policeman get in his way. He runs over them! Think. Think what it mean to have this man on our side, leading us, killing our enemies. The Spider!" Piltsdown tilted back his head and bellowed out a guttural laughter. "The Spider, why Gaucho joost step on him!" Piltsdown's voice

• RICHARD WENTWORTH •

choked off in his throat. Every man there was suddenly a frozen statue of fear.

But Yvonne got softly to her feet and lifted her pert dark face toward the black shadows above. Then they heard the laughter, mocking, hard laughter that bit into their ears like the tocsin of death. When the laughter was finished, words came and the words held the same menace:

"Fools!" it said softly, "do you think to escape the Spider?"

Yvonne's eyes quested back and forth along the running-track balcony, but the voice seemed to come from everywhere. It was not loud, yet it carried to the trembling men below. Piltsdown was the first to recover from the paralysis of fear that seized them. He heaved to his feet, deliberately plucked an automatic from his coat pocket. It seemed tiny in the largeness of his hand.

"Pah!" he exploded. "Show yourself, Spider, if you are not afraid!"

"Certainly," came the Spider's voice. "Where would you like me to show myself?"

He was as courteous as in a drawing room, solicitude in his every word, but still behind it was that mocking hardness.

"Here," said Yvonne clearly. "Here!" She pointed toward the running-track directly opposite the table, not more than thirty feet from where the twelve men were bunched.

"Just a moment," the Spider agreed.

Complete silence fell upon the great hall. Yvonne held her knife in her hand now, and Piltsdown's automatic was ready at his hip. Other men's hands were stealing toward their weapons now.

"Before I show myself," called the Spider, "I have a warning to give you. To any man who allies himself with El Gaucho, I bring certain death! I will not speak again except with bullets. Take heed!"

With his final word, a tiny spot of light from an electric torch glowed into being from the rail of the balcony. It illuminated a man's face beneath the brim of a black hat, a face with a strong, hawk's nose and grim, straight lips; eyes that were black pits….

That spot of light signaled a broadside of gunfire. Thirteen automatics and revolvers blazed lead at that face so deliberately exposed. Their weapons seemed to be hysterically blasting, hiccoughing leaden death in a frenzy of haste. But Yvonne did not hurl her knife. She held it at her side in a white, clenched fist, and her teeth gleamed between drawn-back lips. She did not look long at that illuminated face which a half-hundred leaden slugs were battering. As the guns went empty, she suddenly screamed a warning and jumped toward Piltsdown, striking him violently on the shoulder with both hands to hurl him aside.

Even as she screamed, the laughter of the Spider rang through the hall. The illuminated face on the balcony swayed and spun from side to side as if the Spider had hanged himself there for the bullets of the criminals to strike. Men turned to flee from this hall where a man targeted by scores of bullets still laughed at them tauntingly. Then a shadow swept out of the darkness. A caped figure, with a gun in its right hand, leaped downward in an arc from the edge of the balcony and flung itself directly toward the spot where Oscar Piltsdown tottered on his feet, his massive inertia fighting against the thrust of Yvonne's frantic hands. While the two still struggled there, the Spider swept past them, cape snapping behind him with the wind of his passage. His gun reached out.

There was a crunching thud as his gun-butt slapped against the back of Piltsdown's skull. The blow accomplished what all

Yvonne's pushing had failed to do. It toppled the man off his feet, spilled him headlong across the long table from which all the others had fled. Yvonne was whirled off balance and spun half across the room. She fell to her hands and knees and crouched there like some wild animal, poised to spring.

The Spider sailed on, the whole length of the table, clasping a length of fine, silken line by which he had swung down from the balcony. At the extreme end of his pendulum swing, he released the line, landed lightly on his feet against the wall. He was firing deliberately into the fleeing press at the door and a reloaded weapon was beginning to answer from the fleeing criminals. The darkness which had shielded the Spider before now protected his enemies and Yvonne, recovering herself, lunged toward the table and sent the candles crashing to the floor.

With the darkness, courage seemed to return to the criminals. Their limping fire redoubled and the Spider's gun ceased to answer them. Yvonne's voice rose shrilly.

"He has killed my Oscaire!" she cried. "Kill the Spider! Kill him!"

Her voice broke into a moan, then became sharp again, more determined.

"He must die. The Spider must die," she shrieked. "You let one man rob you of riches! Kill! Kill!"

Lights blazed suddenly as one of the men found the switch. For an instant, guns ceased and there was utter silence, utter blankness in the gymnasium. *The Spider had disappeared!*

CHAPTER 3
DEATH AT THE WHEEL

THE SPIDER heard the thwarted shout that went up from the gymnasium when the men discovered that he had escaped them during the period of darkness. It had been very simple. He had merely climbed back up the silken line by which he had swept down from the balcony to attack and kill Piltsdown. He was stooping to pick up the steel mask which he sometimes wore to conceal his own features in assuming the identity of the Spider, and which he had offered to the men below as a target to draw their bullets.

He heard Yvonne's shriek, "The balcony! You fools, the balcony! He climbed up a rope...."

The Spider's eyes were narrowed as he fled from the balcony. The woman was a shrewd opponent. The fear of the Spider did not affect her, perhaps because she thought her sex exempted her from his vengeance. At any rate, her mind worked clearly in an emergency. He paused a moment in the doorway of the balcony, gun in his hand. The Spider had never slain a woman, but he would not hesitate if his duty demanded that he should—if he deemed it necessary for his defense of humanity. Yvonne drew herself erect above the body of her slain lover, her swelling breasts turned toward the Spider's gun. It was almost as if she saw him there, knew that he stood with weapon tentatively raised.

"Send men to the airport," she cried. "He'll be after Barker now. Hurry, fools!"

17

The Spider leveled his automatic, then cursed raggedly, whirled and raced down the hall. He would probably curse himself many times for not killing the woman, but he could not believe that she would be a serious menace. Men would not listen to her, however shrewd she might be.

She was only the sweetheart of a dead criminal…. But she was right about one thing. He was after this young fool, Barker, who was about to fly westward with the word that would plunge New York into a maelstrom of murder and crime. And he must be fast. Already, he had delayed too long in punishing these minor pawns in the battle. It was some satisfaction to have killed Piltsdown, but first of all now, he must prevent Barker from flying to summon El Gaucho.

The Spider ran silently, on sure feet, an automatic in his right hand, his cape drawn in about him with his left, to prevent it from flapping out a warning of his passage. The Spider had not entered the building without a sure knowledge of its layout and he raced now toward the fire escape which zigzagged across the back of the building, down into a black, unlighted alleyway. Already he could hear the beat of men's feet behind him, racing up to the balcony, scudding up the stairway about the shaft. His pace quickened.

The hallway along which he hastened was straight, lighted by a single red globe at its far end which marked the exit to the fire escape. To his right, three doors at widely spaced intervals gave on the balcony. To his left, there was a series of small dressing rooms lined with lockers. A frown grew on the Spider's forehead as he ran. It became increasingly evident that he would not be able to reach that fire-escape exit before one of his pursuers got sight of him. Damn that girl. If it had not been for her shout....

But there was no time for speculation. He must act—and quickly. Should he risk their seeing him, and defy the accuracy of hostile guns? Or should he duck from sight and attempt an escape later? So far he had not been sighted. There was only the girl's warning cry to set men on his trail.... But, damn it, there was no time to wait. He must escape this building at once and stop Barker, who was already on his way to the airport.

With a grim setting of his lips, Wentworth spun, began to run backward, traveling almost as swiftly as he had with his quiet lope—a heavyweight champion of the prize ring had taught him that trick—and now his gun was ready for the first of his pursuers to show himself. His stratagem was performed just in time. Even as he whirled, two men sprang from a balcony door within twenty feet of him.

THE DOUBLE roar of the Spider's shots sounded almost as a single blast, but the leading man stared at him with a shocked pain in his face, then doubled forward on his face. The second spun sideways, clawed the wall as he slapped down. There was a bloody tear in the back of his coat where it pinched in across the loins. The slapping thunder of the forty-five was still crashing through the building when the Spider reached the exit door and ducked out on the fire escape. Here was no time to affix his tiny mocking death seal to his victims' forehead. Capturing Barker was far more important than hurling that minor mockery into the faces of his enemies.

Caution was cast aside now. The Spider went down the fire-escape steps with great, leaping strides, his heels making the iron ring and ring again. He heard the door above him fling open again, heard a gun crash, but he did not even look upward. The iron slats were closely interlaced above him. They formed an adequate shield. The danger would come later, when he left the protection of the fire escape and raced along the alley toward his car, which would be waiting at the alley's end.

As the Spider whirled along the second-floor platform, he drew back his lips and whistled shrilly between his teeth. His Hindu servant, Ram Singh, who was in the car, undoubtedly would have drawn close on hearing the shots. The whistle would summon him to battle…. But he would have to act swiftly if he were to help. The Spider paused a moment at the end of the second-story platform, leaned out over the rail and slanted three quick bullets upward. They would not wound, but they might frighten…. On the heels of his last shot, he gripped the railing of the fire escape, somersaulted neatly over it and dropped to the ground, diving instantly to the protection of the platform again. He whirled to dart for the street, then shrank back against the wall, smiling.

A low-slung sedan was backing rapidly into the alleyway, its engine roaring between the narrow walls. Ram Singh had indeed caught the signal and was answering as his keen fighting mind directed. The door of the tonneau stopped within inches of the Spider's hand, and he jerked it open, swung in and rapped the glass between him and the Hindu in the same movement. The car lurched forward, hurled the Spider deep into the cushions and rocked into the street on squealing tires.

Even before he righted himself, the Spider snatched the speaking tube. "Newark airport! Fast!" he shouted. "That was well done, O Ram Singh!"

The Spider, disposing himself more comfortably on the cushions, saw the lift of the Hindu's turbaned head, the proud bracing of the shoulders, as if to say, "Does not Ram Singh always serve his master well?"

With a slow smile, the Spider drew out his platinum cigarette case, extracted one of his privately blended smokes and lighted up with a deep inhalation of satisfaction. He began to reload his guns…. The sedan was rocketing through the city, working its way southward across the lights at terrific speed, but with only a low hissing of power from the motor.

The Spider's body was at ease, but his mind raced ahead to the battle that soon must be fought. Although gangster pursuit had not yet developed, he was positive that they would reach Newark airport, where Barker was going, almost as quickly as he. He could forestall them, of course, by phoning police and demanding Barker's arrest at the field, but that would not serve. Even if he was compelled to pursue by plane, the Spider must capture Barker himself. The man had information which the Spider must possess if he were to destroy the criminal alliance in the city and defeat El Gaucho. No, he would take the chance himself, alone. He smiled slightly. Well, the Spider was accustomed to single-handed battle against incredible odds. Deliberately, he picked up the speaking tube again.

He vaulted straight for
the plane's open door!

"Find me a taxi, Ram Singh," he ordered, "then carry this word to the *missie sahib.*"

WENTWORTH OUTLINED then all that he knew about El Gaucho and Tom Barker and the gangsters and knew that Ram Singh would deliver the information perfectly to Nita van Sloan. If anything happened to the Spider in the battle to come, at least his work thus far would not have been in vain. *If anything happened...!* Yes, there was always that possibility for the Spider. He had one defense. When the disguise was removed almost no one knew what manner of man he became. There was Nita and Ram Singh and Jackson, who had been his sergeant during the war and who served him variously now; Jenkyns, his ancient butler. There had been another, Professor Brownlee, mentor of his college days and assistant in scientific matters in later, grimmer days. But one of the master criminals the Spider fought had caused Brownlee's death. The grief was still in the Spider's soul, though he had exacted hundredfold vengeance....

Should he now assume his real identity? The Spider considered while Ram Singh bored southward. His hand dropped to the cushions to his left. A touch on a hidden button there would reveal a secret wardrobe, and disguise equipment in the seat's back, the means of becoming again that dilettante clubman and sportsman which was his real self—that of Richard Wentworth, scion of a wealthy old family of which he was now the sole living member. Slowly, he shook his head. No, that would not do. He must still battle, and it must be as the Spider that he struck.

The sedan ground to a halt beside a taxi and the Spider alighted without a word. His cape hung over his arm now as a coat and his shoulders were straightened to their natural, easy confidence of carriage. His black slouch hat sat more jauntily on his head. But the gaunt, strong-nosed face of the Spider remained. He kept it masked in shadow as he ordered the taxi to speed.

"Newark airport!" he said sharply. "Fifty dollars if you make it in fifteen minutes!"

The cab jumped forward, its motor bellowing, the driver bent forward over the wheel. Wentworth saw his sedan whirl a corner and vanish and knew that within minutes Nita would be receiving Ram Singh's report. His hands strayed to his holstered, reloaded automatics. He would need them soon. Even as his practiced fingers touched the butts, he heard the staccato blast of guns behind and whirled in his seat. No car was roaring in his wake, no stabs of flame heralded an attack. He frowned at the empty street, then faced front again, grim-mouthed.

He knew now what those shots meant. Ram Singh had been attacked in the car the gangsters had trailed. Wentworth's eyes were cold, the set of his lips bitter. He could not return to the faithful Hindu's assistance. The car was bullet-proof, strong as a fort, and the Spider must hasten with his task. His lips tightened even more. It was his code that he followed throughout the wars which racked his heart and soul. Never self, or loved ones; always the service of humanity came first.

The taxi seemed to crawl, though its speedometer wavered always near fifty. It was well after midnight and there was scant traffic, all going very fast. There was a heartbreaking delay when they got a ticket for the Holland tunnel that burrowed under the Hudson River. Two policemen there were talking about El Gaucho. One of them shook a newspaper at the other.

"Look at it!" he said hoarsely. "Two million. Twelve people killed, five of them cops! Suppose that bozo takes it into his head to come here!"

Wentworth bought the paper from the officer for a dollar and read it with scowling eyes while the taxi droned through the tunnel at the required thirty miles an hour.

GAUCHO LOOTS TWO CITIES

So screamed the headlines, and the news explained that a second town forty miles from Jackson City, which had been robbed first, had been struck two hours after the first depredation. Destruction of telephone wires all around had prevented the news from leaking out earlier. The toll in the second town, Harvester, was twenty-two dead. A school bus had got in the way of the escape.

WENTWORTH READ the story with eyes that burned. His jaw clenched until it ached and he felt the hard angry throb of his blood in the knife scar that laid its tracery across his right temple. Soon now he would fly to strike back at El Gaucho.

The cab was speeding now along the elevated motor highway, which bridges the congested cities of northern New Jersey, out to the airport that lay on the southern outskirts of Newark. Minutes dragged past, but finally the field came in sight. They had made incredibly good time. Wentworth was sure Barker could not yet have taken wing.

Thus, the Spider reassured himself as he draped the cape

again about his shoulders and twisted them into those of the hunchback whom all the world knew. He dragged the hat down over his brows, and the taxi swept around the great traffic circle that marked the turn-off to the field.

Even as the cab circled, Wentworth saw a bunched group of men start out from a hangar toward a plane that was warming up on the field. He rapped sharply on the glass.

"Stop!" he ordered, and thrust his gun against the taxi driver's nape.

The man twisted his white frightened face about, dragged on his brakes. Wentworth thrust a hundred-dollar bill into his hand, sprang to the wheel himself, sent the taxi surging forward under its full power. He made no effort to make the long circle that would take him by the regular road to a place behind the hangars, but headed straight for the white, wooden fence that formed the airport's outer boundary. He struck it at forty-five miles an hour, smashed through and roared with increasing speed straight for the plane that the group of men was approaching now....

Seemingly the Spider was driving blindly to attack an anonymous group of men, but he was wise in the way of gangster tactics. He recognized the fighting wedge which they formed with their bodies about a man they protected—knew at first glance that this must be the guard which had been sent to see Barker safely aboard the plane. Within moments, his suspicion was confirmed. An instant after the taxi had crashed through the fence and bounded to the attack, the first bullet sped toward him. It was wild, uncalculated, merely a messenger of defiance. But it was enough to confirm Wentworth's suspicions.

With a hard laugh, the Spider bent over the wheel, spurred the car to its maximum speed. He held the wheel with his left hand, his right clutched his automatic. Deliberately he reached forward, rapped the windshield from its frame, brought splintering glass back into his lap. Better that he knock it out, than that bullets spear it into his face at a crucial moment.

Even after that, the Spider did not open fire. Some of these men he would kill, but there was one he must spare. One of them could help him in his pending battle with El Gaucho, of which this was merely an opening skirmish. Nevertheless, men died as surely in skirmishes as in the most wide-flung battle line. On the Spider charged, and now bullets were flying more thickly. The close group of men had resolved itself into a moving firing-line, four men spread out thinly, behind which another man ran headlong for the waiting plane. Lead pinged off the empty windshield strut, and a second bullet thudded into the upholstery near Wentworth's shoulder.

Once more harsh laughter issued from his lips. He deliberately opened fire. He could distinguish now between the men he wished to kill and the one he would spare. That was sufficient for the Spider. His bullets sped where he willed them to go. At his first shot, one of the four gunmen was straightened out of his crouch, spun about and dropped dead to the ground. Wentworth leveled his automatic again, but abruptly he twisted his head about, held his fire. A new element had entered the battle....

FROM BESIDE the hangars, a motorcycle engine blasted

into action and the machine instantly rolled forward, saddle and sidecar occupied by men in the uniform of State police. Wentworth cursed. He did not battle with the police, regardless of what action they took against him, but they never showed him mercy. If they recognized him, they would discard all effort to apprehend the armed gunmen there who were plotting the nation's destruction and concentrate all their efforts on killing him. The laughter that came from the Spider's lips was bitter now. This was the penalty he paid for his impatience with cumbersome legal machinery. In the eyes of police, he was a murderer, not an executioner of his own swift justice. The price on his head was fifty thousand dollars....

With his eyes grimly set, the Spider fired, once, twice, a third time and the three remaining gangsters went down, like clay pigeons in a shooting gallery. The fifth man, who must be Barker, raced on toward the plane—was almost at the doorway now.

Wentworth held his fire. He did not wish to kill the man, nor to wound him unless it was absolutely necessary. Nor did he wish to disable the plane. It had become, suddenly, his sole hope of escape from this predicament into which his service of mankind had thrown him. The policeman in the sidecar was firing now and with his third shot, a front tire of the taxi flattened with a hissing blast. The two tons of cab went wild, wrenching at the steering gear, lurching in a mad yawing swerve to the left. Wentworth stood up beneath the wheel, fought it with both locked hands, the automatic neglected on the seat beside him. The policeman continued his closely spaced shots.

The Spider, with the desperation of necessity, manhandled

the lurching cab into a reasonably straight course for the plane, now only fifty feet away. Barker was already scrambling into the doorway, and the instant he ducked inside, the plane began to turn its nose into the wind. It would move slowly at first, and would have to run at least two hundred feet on the ground before it lifted. That was the Spider's only hope.

Wentworth whirled the steering wheel desperately, put the steady, spaced firing of police behind him. Now the back of the cab was turned toward the bullets, offering some shelter. The flat tire was pounding, and with a moaning crescendo it ripped loose from the rim and went wobbling off to one side. The cab rode more smoothly now, though the Spider was hard put to hold it to a straight course as he plummeted after the plane. If he could only reach the doorway and hurl himself through it, the pull of the flattened tire on the left front wheel would whirl the taxi away from the plane....

FRANTICALLY, WENTWORTH ground the accelerator to the floor, fighting the clanging pull of the tireless wheel. He was oblivious to the cracking of guns behind him, to the hammer of lead against the car. Only one thing was important—that he catch the plane. Fortunately, in leaping into the ship, Barker had neglected to unhook the door that was fastened open against the side of the plane. But the powerful slipstream of the racing propellers was battling to tear it loose. The door jerked at its fastenings.

Wentworth's shoulders ached with the wrenching strain of the wheel, but his eyes remained calm and clear. He saw exactly what he must do and estimated his chances narrowly. He was even with the tail of the ship now, but it was rapidly gaining headway. Even as Wentworth drew abreast, the tail lifted. Another hundred feet and the plane's wheels would lift from the earth and moments later, it would pull upward. Then there would be no chance left for the Spider at all.

Before this deathly chase had begun, he had hopes of pursuing by plane if he were too late to intercept Barker, but that was ruined now. If he failed to catch the ship, not only would be have no chance at all to catch the man, but no hope even of living! For the taxi's steering-gear would not stand up much longer under the fearful punishment of high speed and crippled wheels; the motorcycle was rapidly overhauling him. Soon the police guns could not miss. And he could not fire on agents of the law, even if it meant his own death....

These thoughts flashed through Wentworth's mind as he gave the last of his ability and strength to the task of overtaking the ship. He crawled ahead steadily, but slowly—oh, so slowly! Once the plane left earth... He was still ten feet behind the doorway when he saw the tires lift slightly for the first bound. He was straining forward, as if with his own weight he would lend the taxi additional speed. A bullet whined past his ear. He was no longer laughing, but there was a smile on his mouth, a tight-lipped smile that matched the hard, cold gleam of his eyes. He must make it, *he must!*

Only seven feet to gain, now only five. Wentworth jerked the hand throttle of the taxi to the last notch, caught the wheel with his left hand and eased out from under it. He had to strain frantically to hold the cab one-handed while he got into a position to spring. The plane's wheels were lifting again, even more lightly. Three feet now before he would be opposite the doorway; three feet that might well be his doom. He stooped cautiously, caught up his automatic and pocketed it. Even in his extremity, he did not forget that. He had dozens of automatics, perfectly matched for balance and barrel, all registered in different identities, but the particular pair he carried now were in his own name. No, these must not fall into the hands of the police. The wheels of the plane lifted finally from the earth, just skimming it, but clear, none the less. Within seconds, it would be battling its way toward the skies. Now, at last there was only a scant foot of difference in the doorways of taxi and plane. Wentworth could wait no longer. He braced himself, released the cab's wheel at the same instant that he vaulted high into the air and sprang straightaway for the open door of the plane.

In the split second of time while he hung suspended there in the air, empty hands outstretched toward the sides of the ship, he saw two things. The door was tearing loose from its fastenings and swinging violently downwind, as if evilly inspired, as if to slam in Wentworth's face or strike him from the precarious hold which he sought. He saw, too, that Barker, his face desperately white, stood braced in the doorway, his hands balled in fists, to knock him loose if he should gain a momentary grip on the door frame. And either one would mean the Spider's death. Taxi and plane were both making sixty miles an hour. A plunge to the hard earth at that terrific speed would smash every bone in his body. And if he survived that, there were the police…!

CHAPTER 4
BATTLE IN THE SKY

I F THERE had been time, in that brief moment when he flew through the air, Wentworth would have screamed defiance, would have laughed aloud. His courage was indomitable, his will supreme. He drew his feet forward, doubled his legs under his body and catapulted into the narrow open space of the doorway at the same instant the slipstream of the propellers slammed the door shut. The door caught him on his back and its impetus pitched him against the man who stood with clenched fists to hammer him back to his death. Together they rolled across the narrow width of the cabin. Wentworth felt the plane yaw beneath him, stagger with the weight of his leap. Its wheels banged against the earth. Then the whole ship shuddered its way upward to steadiness again.

The Spider was more than half-stunned by the violence of his entrance, but with the trained reflexes of his remarkable body, he was on his feet almost instantly, battling against Barker's attack, while his mind reeled from shock. His guns stayed in their holsters. He had not struggled this far to keep this man alive only to kill him at the end of the chase. He knew at least that there would be no help for Barker from the pilot, even if the man were armed. His hands would be busy getting the ship aloft after that narrow escape close to the earth.

Gradually as he fought, clinching, warding off blows, his head cleared and from behind his lifted arms, he looked into the face of the man he battled. The whiteness of fear was gone from

Tom Barker's cheeks, and there was something almost merry in the twinkling of his brown eyes that was strangely familiar to Wentworth. The man was young, not more than twenty-three, and had a remarkably high and well-developed forehead. His face was round, almost chubby, and his mouth, smiling now, had the determination, the strength of an older man for all its young cheerfulness. Tousled brown hair lay in curly clusters close to his head.

Wentworth's remarkable stamina had pulled him completely out of his daze now, but before the hard hammer of the younger man's fists, he feigned hurt, wobbling even more on his feet, retreating stumblingly until he got the position he wanted. Barker's young enthusiasm misled him. He bored in for the knockout and Wentworth's left lanced out to the face, pulling Barker up short, straightening him for the knockout right that came whistling in at exactly the right heartbeat of time. Barker arched backward, stumbled and thumped down supine in the aisle, eyes closed, out cold....

The Spider stooped slowly, picked up his hat, set it on his head. His chest was heaving with his exertions, his heart pumping hard and swiftly in his throat, but he did not delay. He made his way forward, opened the door behind the pilot and met the man's frightened stare as he pulled his chin about on his shoulder.

"This ship has been re-chartered," Wentworth told him dryly. "There's a small landing field at Bedford, New York. Head for it."

A trembling jerked at the pilot's shoulders; his face was drawn, and words gurgled in his throat.

"The Spider!" he gasped. "The Spider!"

Wentworth nodded gravely. "Quite so. You have my instructions?"

"Yes, sir. Yes, sir!"

Wentworth nodded again, found that the pilot was unarmed, and shut the door on the cockpit as he turned back to Barker. The man was stirring on the floor of the cabin. The Spider dropped into a seat near him, gravely lighted a cigarette while he waited for Barker to recover consciousness entirely. There was a quiet satisfaction in Wentworth's movements. He was rapidly throwing off the exhaustion of the pursuit, his gray-blue eyes were hawklike and keen beneath the black brim of his hat. He removed the hat slowly, laid it on the seat opposite him and revealed the smooth, high reach of his forehead which even the sinister disguise of the Spider could not conceal.

THERE WAS a kindliness in his eyes now that seemed strange in a man of so savage a reputation. The men he had killed were numbered somewhere in the police files of a hundred cities in half the nations of the world. Somewhere, too, in secret archives, Nita had kept account of them. They ran into high hundreds, and each had died for some evil deed, for some fierce crime against humanity or against some innocent individual. But Wentworth's eyes were not those of a killer. They were keenly intelligent, warmly human. In his natural face, in repose, there was a touch of sadness, of the universal grieving for mankind which no language can express so well as the German *Weltschmerz*. But now, there was a gentle humor in his face, too.

He had come after Barker, prepared to find him a brutal criminal, such a man as might well represent so great a killer, so murderous a robber as this El Gaucho. Instead, he had found a youngster whose eager fighting smile might well match the Spider's own. There was something clean about the boy, clean and healthy. The Spider was suddenly glad that he had not killed him.

Barker stirred again on the floor, lifted a hand to his jaw and breathed out a sound that was almost a moan. He sat up abruptly, looked at Wentworth. His eyes widened at sight of the sinister garb and face; then their eyes met and, slowly, uncertainly, Barker smiled.

"Man!" he said. "You sure pack a wallop!"

Wentworth did not smile. When he smiled in his disguise, it did sinister things to his face as it was meant to, but his eyes remained kindly.

"It's necessary sometimes," he replied briefly. "How did you get yourself involved with that band of criminals. I almost killed you."

Barker was silent for a dozen heartbeats, staring up into Wentworth's face. His cheeks drained of color and an involuntary shudder touched his shoulders. Then he smiled sheepishly. "I'm not a coward," he said, "but… the way you say that! I can almost… *feel* death. Who are you?"

Wentworth looked down at his captive speculatively. When he questioned men, he frequently terrified them with a sight of the red seal which he so often placed upon the dead foreheads of the victims of his swift justice, but there was a clear intelligence in the eyes of this man that struck a sudden chord of sympathy in Wentworth's heart. He leaned forward a little, elbows on his knees.

"The Spider," he answered simply.

Barker caught his breath, but there was no terror in his eyes, and Wentworth was glad of his decision—pleased again that he had not shot him. His lack of fear was the surest proof of his complete honesty. Wentworth was suddenly sure that Barker had had no criminal part in the negotiations between the New York criminals and El Gaucho.

Wentworth said calmly, "I can see that you have no fear of me, and you are right. The Spider never harms an innocent man. However, you have certainly placed yourself in an incriminating position. I think you would do well to explain in detail just what happened to you that you got mixed up with that crowd."

Barker pushed himself to his feet, dropped into a seat facing Wentworth. "You're right. I want to thank you for getting me out of a damned bad jam." He leaned forward, elbows on his knees. "I'll come clean, but it's a crazy story. It will be hard for you to believe."

Wentworth offered his cigarette case and, after they had both lighted up, asked gravely, "Why not try me?"

Barker nodded eagerly, his brown eyes serious and intent. "My father and mother are dead," he began. "A few months ago, my grandfather was killed by some crooks here in New York. I was in C.C.C. camp at the time and as soon as I could, I came east. Hitchhiked. I thought I'd give some other guy a chance in the camp and maybe granddad would have left me enough to live on. I found a guy named Wentworth was executor, but I couldn't reach…."

Wentworth could not prevent the start that jerked at his muscles, but his face betrayed nothing at all. He stared at Barker and forced himself to calmness, made his voice slow.

"This grandfather of yours who was killed—who was he?"

There was a choking in Wentworth's throat. He looked again at the man's brown, alert eyes, his high, intelligent forehead, and was sure in advance that he knew what the answer would be. An old grief rose up to overwhelm him, and there was a dryness in his eyes that made them sting.

Barker looked up, a little surprised at the interruption. "Why," he said slowly, "his name was Brownlee, a professor he was, and…."

Wentworth came to his feet. "Professor Brownlee!"

HE HAD been right then! The certainty that he had hesitated to phrase in his own mind overwhelmed him. This man was the grandson of Professor Brownlee, the cheerful old man who had been his closest associate through the years of his battling against the Underworld, the man who had been a father to him in his parentless days, who had died fighting the Spider's battle. No wonder he had taken so instantly to this youngster who had so many brave features of the old professor. It was rarely that any happening could pierce the hard composure that had many times been Wentworth's sole protection against his enemies, but this sudden discovery of Professor Brownlee's grandson… Wentworth remembered now that Professor Brownlee had had a daughter who had died a while after the Spider had been born… He found himself gripping Barker's hand hard, looking into brown, slightly puzzled eyes.

"He was a great—a brave—man, that grandfather of yours," Wentworth said, pushing down his emotion. "I am proud to know his grandson."

Tom Barker smiled. They both sat down again. Wentworth became preoccupied with lighting a cigarette. Barker said eagerly, "Then you knew him?"

Wentworth shook his head. "Wentworth and I frequently fight the same battles," he said quietly. "There have been times when we helped one another. Professor Brownlee was one of Wentworth's most intimate associates, helped him out in his fights. That's how he was killed. A great man."

While Barker went on with his story then, Wentworth watched him covertly, seeing anew resemblances to his old friend. That certain quick way of moving his hands in a gesture, that occasional up-looking cheerful glance, the merriness that lurked in his eyes. Yes, there could be no mistake. It was remarkable that he had himself not noticed the resemblance….

Barker's story was simple enough. He had been hitchhiking his way to New York and had happened to be in a city that El Gaucho raided. When he arrived in New York, he had been unable to get in touch with Wentworth—the Spider had been busy in the Underworld and Wentworth had been "away on a trip"—and he had managed to sell his story of El Gaucho to a newspaper as a means of supporting himself until Wentworth returned. Afterward, the police had come for him and he had run away in fright. Yvonne Musette had found him and taken him to see Piltsdown....

"I had to repeat my brag then, sir," he said, looking up at Wentworth, "or it would have gone hard with me. My brag, I mean, that I could find El Gaucho any time I wanted to...."

"Can you, Tom?"

Barker grinned. "Of course not. But Piltsdown believed I could, chiefly because he wanted to. He surrounded me with his gunmen and I had no choice but to do what they wanted. I didn't want to die yet a while, especially..." His voice died, his cheeks reddened a little. Wentworth waited patiently, but he did not continue. He went on with another line of talk. The Spider felt a sharp disappointment at learning that Barker's story of being able to find El Gaucho was false, but his curiosity was aroused by his awkward lapse into silence, his flush. Finally, he penetrated Barker's reserve.

"Well, sir," Barker said slowly, "it's like this. I'm kind of ashamed of anything so kiddish, but there it is and I can't change it. When El Gaucho raided this town, I saw a girl with him, and... and, damn it, sir, I won't be happy until I see her again!"

Wentworth frowned down at his hands. A memory came back to him, a memory that stretched across years. In those days, the Spider was a new terror across the red skies of the Underworld, an angel of sudden death. One night, bowing suavely in a friend's home, above a white hand among so many white hands, Wentworth had looked up into eyes that were violet and warmly deep... *Damn it, sir, I won't be happy until I see her again*... Strange that he should feel so close to this boy, this man.

40

Wentworth said dryly, "You'll probably be better off if you never see her again. Now, you must talk fast. We'll land in a few minutes. I want to know how El Gaucho works, and what Piltsdown and his crowd are planning…."

BARKER HARKED back to the girl.

"You'll think it awfully funny, sir, about the girl, when I tell you what this Gaucho does. Why, I saw him push his gun up against an old man's throat and blow a hole through it. He almost tore his head off, sir, and here I am thinking about a girl that was with him."

Wentworth's jaw hardened beneath its firm skin and his lips parted in a smile that was not pleasant to see.

"Tell me more of this Gaucho," he said softly.

Barker looked at the Spider's face and a shudder touched his shoulders. "I'd like to be with you, sir, when you kill him," he said simply. He sat silent for a full minute, staring down at his brown, calloused hands, began abruptly to talk.

"Gaucho's men all dress in yellow slickers and they cover their heads with red hoods so nobody can see their faces. They wear a band of scarlet and purple around their left arms.

"They have all kinds of guns. They shoot everybody they see on sight. I think the girl saved my life. I was in a doorway staring at them and a man looked my way and the girl rode her horse in front of me. I think she saved my life."

"El Gaucho, Barker," the Spider prompted softly.

"Yes, sir. Well, I saw a man fire a shotgun at him from fifteen feet away and it didn't hurt him. He killed the man and kept on shooting him after he was on the ground. One of the men threw a girl across his horse, a kid that couldn't any more than have finished high school. I chased him, but he shot at me, got clean away. They set the town on fire before they left."

Wentworth's eyes were gray-blue flame. His voice still came softly, but there was an edge like surgical steel to his words.

"Now, tell me about Piltsdown."

The anger still flamed in Wentworth's face when Barker had finished, but there was a frown on his forehead and an impatience in his every gesture. He was on fire to battle this Gaucho, but he knew that the fight might well be long, and Barker's story of Piltsdown and his plans had made it plain that the Spider's first duty was to the city. The alliance that was planned reached to the last rat-hole of the Underworld and would weld all its sly, poisonous strength into a machine that would throttle mankind within a few months. They would truly, as Piltsdown had said, "own the city" within weeks.

No, it was plain that he must strike first here in New York City, destroy this festering terror before the leaders could bring this super-bandit here for the Underworld to acclaim emperor. Once more, he must delay his trip westward. With that decision, a new grimness settled upon the Spider. How could one man hope to cope with so widespread and powerful an organization? Lop off the head? He smiled bitterly. That sanguinary activity would probably entail first battling his way through the entire army of El Gaucho!

Wentworth leaned to the window and saw that the field toward which the pilot slanted the plane was empty in the gray light of early dawn. He turned back to Barker, took out a blank card and swiftly scribbled a note and an address upon it, signed it with the Spider's seal.

"This lady is a friend of Wentworth," he said. "You will be cared for until he returns. By all means, keep clear of Yvonne Musette and her crowd."

Barker smiled wryly, "You can count on that sir, if I see them first!"

Wentworth nodded slowly. The plane set down lightly on the field, taxied to one of the two small hangars on the edge of the narrow macadam road that led past, killed the motor. Wentworth left the plane, taking Barker with him in an automobile they rented from a caretaker on the field. On the edge of the city, they parted. Wentworth clasped Barker's hand.

"Go to that address," he said, "and I can assure you your troubles will be over."

Barker seemed reluctant to release his hand. "But you, sir? When will I see you again? Where are you going?"

The Spider smiled and his eyes were no longer friendly to lighten its sinister aspect. "I am paying a call on these erstwhile friends of yours."

"But not alone?"

Wentworth laughed. He thrust Barker from the car, made it roar down the street, leaving the man standing there on the curb. He laughed again, softly, as he raced southward toward the rendezvous that had been arranged for Tom Barker, bearing the answer of El Gaucho. The Spider would keep that appointment... bearing death!

CHAPTER 5
RENDEZVOUS OF DEATH

T HE PLACE of rendezvous was another—though much
smaller—athletic club. Wentworth wondered grimly if
Piltsdown had control over every such place in New York City.
He realized at once, however, the advantages for Piltsdown of
such an establishment. Men of all sorts could go to the clubs
without question and that would afford facility of contact with
the underlings which he must have.

The criminals would be present, all right. According to Barker's information, there was always a large force there and tonight
the leaders would be panicky over the Spider's successes. They
would keep together for strength and courage. Was it mad for
one man to plan such an invasion single-handed? Perhaps, but
Wentworth had gone many times into such traps and come out
alive and triumphant. True, this time he would have no rear
guard, no second line of defense, such as Ram Singh, lurking in
the background to catch his signal, or attempt rescue if something went wrong....

Speeding the slatternly touring car, Wentworth felt an abrupt
reversal of his feeling of self-confidence. It was as if some inner
warning had been sounded, as if Death had blown its fetid
breath in his face, laughing as it held out bony hands of welcome.
Wentworth tried to shrug the feeling aside, but it persisted. He
repeated to himself steadily that he had conquered against much
greater odds and when the reiteration brought no relief from
gloom, he thrust the whole aside, relegated it to the back of his

mind. It did not matter that apprehension bestrode his shoulders…. One concession he made to his dread. He stopped at an all-night drug store and, carrying his cape, cocking his hat, went into a phone booth to call Nita van Sloan. He knew she would be awake. When the Spider roved abroad, she did not sleep until he had come, as he invariably did, to her studio apartment high above the Hudson on Riverside Drive.

When her quiet contralto sang to him over the wire, Wentworth closed his eyes for a long moment, but when he spoke, his voice was vigorous and confident as he knew so well how to make it.

"Nita, darling," he whispered.

Nita cried, "Dick, you rascal, why didn't you call me sooner?"

They laughed together then and there was more talk, but Wentworth stopped that soon and told Nita rapidly what had transpired since Ram Singh had left him. His faithful Hindu, he learned, had eluded the attack after giving the pursuing gangsters a brief battle.

"I'm sending Barker to you," Wentworth told Nita briskly. "He should be there in an hour or so. I imagine he'll be dubious about coming before eight o'clock anyway. I'm on my way now, Nita, my sweet. Yes, of course I'll be careful… See you soon…."

Wentworth hung up the receiver and stood for a long moment with his head hanging, his eyes closed. That *See you soon* had cost him a pang. He could say that when the presentiment of disaster was cold within him, but he could not deceive himself. Abruptly, his head came up. Was this the Spider who could talk and think such things? Nonsense. The Spider had always won. Always

NITA VAN SLOAN

would. There could be no defeat for him. At least, there should be no thought of defeat....

He reentered the car, sped on southward, presently braked to a halt a block from the building of the rendezvous and sat silently studying it. About him, the early traffic of New York was beginning to rumble, a few street cars were rattling, clanging past; motorists hurrying home from all-night tasks or speeding to early work; bums awaking from their doorway beds and shuffling along with sagging shoulders and sleep-fuddled heads. The last, dreary street-washing truck was lumbering home with its spray nozzles dribbling water. And the streets were still dirty with the litter of last night's crowds. This was Broadway after sunrise, with its glittering signs extinguished by the dawn and the garishness of its tawdry night ashamed by daylight. The rendezvous was at Forty-fifth and Broadway, a basement athletic club. The building was fourteen or fifteen stories high, with entrances on two streets. Wentworth took the only possible course, walking straight up to the main door.

INSIDE THE double barrier of glass, the night watchman was red-eyed but awake, waiting for his relief. At Wentworth's sharp rap on the outer door, the man ambled forward, but with a hand lifted to the neck of his vest where gunmen, but rarely watchmen, carry weapons. Wentworth saw all this with eyes that seemed utterly disinterested, his manner impatient. He guessed

that, even as he had expected, the guard was one of Piltsdown's own men. Surely, the leader would not have trusted so important a post to anyone not in his employ.

Wentworth rapped again on the door, gesturing sharply to the man. The watchman's face wrinkled but he shuffled forward more rapidly, fumbled one-handed with the locks while he still peered through the glass, keeping a hand near his gun. Wentworth leaned toward the glass, gestured with his hands to hold the man's attention and got a knee against the door. As he heard the bolt of the lock slip back, he threw all his weight against the portal, slamming it inward and hurling the watchman backward off-balance. Before the man's gun was half-drawn, Wentworth had reached his side and thrust his stiffened fingers against the man's throat, dropping him unconscious to the floor.

It was the work of a moment to latch the door again, to drag the night watchman into the elevator and allow the gate to slide shut. He would be safe there until he recovered consciousness, which would be at least a half hour from now. No one could open the door from the outside without a special key. Wentworth smiled slightly to himself as he made his way silent-footed down the stairs. If all his victories were as simple as this one…. Halfway down he paused. It seemed to his tautly attuned ears that he had heard a footstep in the hall above, which should contain only the unconscious watchman. His smile thinning, he drew his cape about his shoulders, palmed his two automatics. It was barely possible that his return had been anticipated.

The stairway he was descending was marble and broad. It reached to the basement in three short flights describing three sides of a square. Wentworth was in the middle of the second flight now, and from his position, he could see both the head and the foot of the stairway, plus a section of the basement hall. There were two doors with upper panels of ground glass within view. Only darkness was behind them, but the corridor itself was dimly lighted by widely spaced electric bulbs. There was no repetition of the sound above and presently, the Spider drifted on downward. His eyes were wary.

He did not believe it possible that he had miscalculated, that the allies of Piltsdown would not be here in this basement rendezvous. Yet nothing stirred about him; there was no light or indication of life. Wentworth's disguised face became a hard mask. His certainty of a trap increased. At the foot of the stairs he paused. One corner of the upper hallway was still in view. He weighed his guns in his hands while he watched it. He wondered if he were allowing the premonition which had chilled him before his entrance to play tricks on him. But there was no answer except the weighty silence of the building about him. Slowly Wentworth's lips lifted from his teeth. The Spider had come here to kill! Deliberately, he lifted his left hand gun and blasted out the single light bulb that was in sight. His eyes flicked to it only for a heartbeat, then they were focused again on that corner of the upper hall. Hard on the heels of the crashing shot, a man sprang into view up there in the hallway above, racing for the stairs, a gun in his hand. Wentworth's right-hand automatic blasted and the man's head jerked. His gun hand half-lifted with a queer, wooden stiffness. But it did not quite level. In the midst of deliberate movement, the man's body went

abruptly limp and he pitched in a
heap down the first flight of stairs,
landed with a sodden thump on the
second platform above Wentworth.
THE SPIDER pressed close
against the wall at the corner of the
hall and watched the two doors he

could see, glanced now and again at that corner of the hallway
above. The echo of his shots could not fail to have roused someone. It was his one course of action. Barker had not known the
layout of the club, so he could only launch the attack and so
draw the leaders to him.

Still no sound reached his waiting ears. The corridor seemed
to be empty even of the echo of his shots. Wentworth's eyes
narrowed on one of the glass doors. Abruptly, he sprang forward,
casting a quick glance up and down the hallway as he moved. No
one was in sight. Wentworth put his shoulders against the wall
between the two doors and listened again. He was almost certain
he had glimpsed movement behind that ground glass panel.

Suddenly, without warning, the silence of the hallway was
shattered by a blasting roar. He saw the glass panel of the door
to his right smash to the floor, but its fall was soundless in the
greater, overwhelming chatter of a machine gun. With a sensation of cold that crept up the flesh of his back, Wentworth saw
the bullets claw the wall at the corner where, a brief moment
before, he had stood. They splashed white powder from the
marble steps, scored black holes in the plaster.

He crouched, ready for action. When the machine gun stammered into surprised silence, Wentworth sprang past the doorway. He was visible for only a heartbeat to those inside, but in that speck of time, Wentworth had fired twice. His cape whipped backward from his shoulders and before it was clear, the machine gun roared again. The Spider felt the lead tug at his cape, but through its chatter came a sound that was between a gasp and a moan. The machine gun ceased its angry cackle and a man's footsteps, slapping heavily on the floor in flight, echoed from the room.

The Spider nodded. His bullets had sped truly once more. He sprang past the doorway once more, saw that the room was empty except for a dead man who lay hunched grotesquely over his silent machine gun. Wentworth moved quietly into the room, while his eyes quested about. He opened the base of each of his guns in turn and reloaded from a supply of cartridges he carried loose in his pocket. It was clearly a waiting room, with hard benches against the wall and, in the corner, a box of an office with a windowlike cashier's cage.

Thoughtfully, Wentworth holstered his automatics and eased the machine gun out from under the dead man. The man had an extra drum of ammunition beside him and the one on the gun was only half-emptied. Wentworth nodded his satisfaction and, the machine gun cradled against his hip, went toward the door where the other fugitive gunman had disappeared. The room beyond was empty, but as the Spider sprang sideways through the doorway, seeking instantly the cover of the wall, an automatic banged through the letter slot of a door directly opposite it.

Wentworth drummed out a short burst in answer, heard bullets clang upon the slot and hit with a flat, dull ring upon the door. He recognized the sound. The door was steel, impregnable to his bullets. But the lead that he had fanned through the letter slot had gone true, for the automatic ceased. His face alight with eagerness for the battle, he crossed the room in long strides, set the muzzle of the machine gun against the slot and swept it in an arc across the room beyond, which he could not see. Men's screams came clearly through the steel portal, their shrillness rising even above the deafening clangor of the gun.

UNTIL THE last bullet sped from the barrel, Wentworth held the gun to the slot, then he ran lightly back across the room, detaching the spent drum, snapping new ammunition into place. By the time he reached the hallway again, the machine gun was once more cradled against his hip. As he sprang from the door, he caught a fragmentary glimpse of two men crouching down the stairs with revolvers in hand. They fired first, but they fired wildly. The machine gun moved six inches, vibrating with the roll of its discharge, and both men crumpled down the last few steps to the floor.

Over their bodies, Wentworth paused for a moment, touching the base of his gleaming platinum cigarette case to their foreheads. When he straightened, a small splotch of richest vermilion glowed there, a miniature symbol of sprawling hairy legs and poised venomous fangs, *the seal of the Spider!* These were not the men he had wanted to kill tonight, but they would do, to start. Certain it was that they were hirelings of the crowd which sought to rule the city and bring El Gaucho here with his murderous cruelty and his ruthless looting.

A slow fire of anger was burning within Wentworth's breast. The leaders were keeping hidden, damn them, sending their killers to battle in their stead. But the Spider would find them, track them down. He went along the hallway on slow, silent feet, deliberate as death, the gun cradled against his hip. He saw then, for the first time, a lighted doorway. The light had not been there before when he had sprung across the corridor. Of that he was certain. But it glowed brightly now like a trap for unwary moths.

The Spider went grimly toward it, the machine gun ready. To him, that light was a challenge and he was suddenly sure that it had been intended for precisely that. Indeed, as he watched, the door swung wide and a man, back turned toward him, sauntered away from it into the lighted room. He took a seat at a long table. Four other men about the table were visible, but all remained motionless. Wentworth continued his advance until he stood in that lighted doorway and saw the whole table. Its head was occupied by Yvonne Musette.

The hands of every one of the men were in sight on the table and none held a gun. Yvonne's hands were visible, too. She held a fountain pen poised over a sheet of paper that was half-covered with her writing. She smiled jauntily at the Spider as he came slowly over the sill. He was wary for trickery and stepped immediately clear of the doorway so that he should not be taken from behind. This was nothing that he had expected, this apparent abject surrender, but he stood, confidently smiling, with the vicious snout of the machine gun sweeping those white-faced men about the table. There was no mistaking their terror. The sweat of fear beaded their foreheads and its power was palsying their clenched hands. Only the woman seemed fearless, her red lips curved in mockery. Wentworth's eyes went beyond the table. He was covered from no doorway, nor hidden window.

Yvonne got to her feet, still with that mocking smile on her lips. She toyed with the pen still in her tapering, small hands.

"Please, M'sieur Spider," she said, "do you give quarter when your prisoners surrendaire?"

Wentworth's attention focused on the fountain pen in her hands, and a tension gripped all his muscles. Like lightning, his machine gun's muzzle swung about, toward the woman, but he knew even as he moved that he was too late. A queer, hoarse cry sprang to his lips. He saw powder flame blaze from the end of the fountain pen and that flame set fire to his brain. Great red-and-white lights exploded within his skull. He thought, I knew I would curse myself for not killing her. She shot me with a fountain-pen pistol. After that, nothingness....

AS YVONNE Musette was Wentworth's last conscious thought, so the sense of her nearness was the first thing in his mind when he began to recover. He became aware of her voice, imploring at first, then raging. She was shouted down by a man. Wentworth moved his hands gently and found them bound; found, also, that all his clothing had been stripped from his upper body. He shifted his legs a little and they were naked, too, and bound. He opened his eyes, then—no need to pretend further—and looked into a circle of men's hating faces. Yvonne was outside the circle, struggling to get in, sobbing now.

"Please, please let me keel him," she begged. "Can't you understan'? He keel Oscaire and he keel Tommy Barkaire, too. It ees my righ' to keel him!"

There was the sound of a blow, and a man with a mocking voice said: "If you don't shut up, Yvonne, I'll have to do something about it." He spoke very gently, but with a fierce enjoyment half concealed in his tones. Yvonne's voice broke into French, cursing violently, then stopped suddenly. Wentworth studied the man who had spoken. He was six feet three or four, with a narrow head topped by smooth, black hair, his whole body extremely thin. His face was lean, in character with the general skinniness of his body, and it held a wolfish look when he smiled. There was something about the eyes, too, so wide open that the whites almost showed above the iris....

Wentworth said slowly, "How are you, Peterson? I scarcely know whether to welcome or resent your protection...."

The wolfish smile drew up the thin man's lip corners tautly. "Greetings, Spider! It would be much better for you, I imagine, if you resented it." He squatted on his heels so he could look into Wentworth's face more closely. There was gloating in his wide-open eyes. "So that you will be better able to judge, I'll explain just what's in store for you. You will know from the fact that we have stripped you, and by my reprimand of Yvonne, that we intend to keep you prisoner for a while. You are so neat in your escapes, Spider, that I have devised a special prison for you—but more of that a little later.

"Meantime—" the man's face opened in his grin again—"meantime we are going to send word to El Gaucho

55

again—through the newspapers so that there will be no slip-up. We are going to tell him that we have the Spider and are holding him prisoner for his disposal. What do you think El Gaucho will do to you, eh, Spider?"

Wentworth lay quite still, the smile on his disguised face sinister and ugly. "That's very nice of you," he said softly. "That's just what I've been waiting for—to meet El Gaucho!"

Peterson laughed and his mirth, like his speaking voice, sounded gentle. "But not the way you will meet him, Spider. This Gaucho is a murdering madman, from all I can hear, and he won't be too pleasant with you." He stared at Wentworth speculatively. "Too bad you won't be around to see the fun. Can you imagine, Spider, the Gaucho taking New York like he took Jackson City this afternoon? Looting every bank in town; smacking down the police; burning the houses that get in his way. By God, Spider, think of New York on fire! You may see that before long, when El Gaucho comes…. Only I forgot. *Pardon* my laughter. *You* won't see it."

HE STRAIGHTENED and, at his signal, two men lifted the Spider, one at his shoulders and one at his feet, and carried him, staggering, into a hall and along that to another door. Wentworth saw that he was still in the basement athletic club which he had entered to destroy these same criminals. Then police had not heard the shooting? The gun explosions must have been muffled by more than merely being underground. Well, it didn't matter. Apparently the soundproofing had been adequate….

Yvonne's voice broke out sharply again. "Do you know that

this Spider killed eleven of our men?" she cried hoarsely. "Eleven men here tonight!"

"I've been told," said Peterson lazily, "that the Gaucho has ways of taking care of such men. Now shut up, Yvonne!"

Wentworth was taken through a short hall into a tiled room with a small swimming pool, really nothing more than a plunge. He was thrust painfully into a chair and straps and ropes wound about him until they cut into the flesh. Wentworth maintained a curious smile throughout the entire proceedings.

"You see," explained Peterson, "you have *quite* a reputation for escapes. Still, I don't believe that you will be able to get out of this one. The chair is heavily weighted and you will be put in water up to your chin. The water may loosen the ropes a little, but there are handcuffs and leather belts in addition to those. You get the idea?"

The Spider nodded pleasantly. "It should be quite effective," he murmured politely. "May I congratulate you on your arrangements?"

Peterson bowed, but there was a slightly worried look in his eyes. It was as if the Spider's nonchalance had given Peterson the idea of some secret resource. Roughly, he searched Wentworth's body for some hidden implement of escape, but he found nothing. There was nothing to find. Peterson stepped back finally, satisfied.

"There will be no guard," he said. "I think that will be safer."

"It really must be quite a reputation I have," Wentworth murmured.

At Peterson's signal, four of the men caught up the chair

and held it over the edge of the pool, began slowly to lower it toward the surface. The water was chill and its first shock raced up through Wentworth's legs from his feet. He smiled up at Peterson.

"Come on in," he said, "the water's fine… after you get used to it!"

Peterson's wolfish smile lifted his mouth corners. He said nothing, and the chair dipped lower into the water. It washed about Wentworth's thighs now, and something that was colder than the water was in his breast. Its name was despair. He knew how well Peterson had planned. The first move to escape from a chair was to throw the chair to the floor, so as to change the stress on the ropes. If he tried that in the water….

"I hope you've calculated the depth of the water well," he called cheerfully. "I doubt if a dead Spider would appeal to El Gaucho."

"Tried it out on myself," Peterson assured him and lifted a hand to his throat. "Right up to here!"

Wentworth drew in a swift breath. If Peterson were telling the truth…! He felt the water wash his throat and still the chair was sinking. He stretched his chin upward. His entrance into the plunge had caused a small wave that rippled up the other end of the pool, then back again. It slapped him in the mouth. Water that came up to Peterson's larynx would be over Wentworth's chin, lapping at his mouth! He would have to stretch his neck, strain his head backward to escape drowning!

Finally, Wentworth felt the legs of the chair touch bottom. His head was tilted far back and his mouth was just clear of the water. When the small wave rippled back again, it covered his mouth and nostrils and ears. Peterson stooped at the side of the pool and splashed a handful of water into the Spider's face.

"Why don't you say something nonchalant now, Spider?" he jeered, sloshing water again.

WENTWORTH CAUGHT a gasped breath just before the spray hit him, held it while that wave covered his mouth. Presently it would be still and Wentworth could breathe without interruption. As long as his neck could stand the strain....

Deliberately, Wentworth lowered his head. When it was in normal position, the water came above his eyes. He kept his eyes just above the surface and looked into Peterson's face. Without malevolence, without any expression at all except mild amusement. Peterson cursed, jerked to his feet and shouted at the others about him.

"Get out of here! Go on, get out!" They moved sluggishly, glancing back in fascination at the black head that just topped the water. Wentworth lifted his head and sucked in a deep breath, lowered his chin again so that his eyes were just above water. There was a rigid calm in his face, but the chill that was all about his body was creeping into his heart—into his very soul. How long were they going to keep him immersed like this? Until El Gaucho could come east? But that might be days! Something like panic thrust through Wentworth like a sword. He jerked his head back, straining head and nostrils above the water, breathing shallowly and fast. Better to drown himself at once than wait for the inevitable exhaustion....

Bitterly, Wentworth fought for calmness. He was not, he

instructed himself, concerned with personal survival. What he must do was to live to triumph over El Gaucho and prevent the disastrous raid that marauder would certainly make on New York as soon as he accepted their invitation to come and lead them. The Spider had no personal life, no personal rights to die. Strangely, this thought steadied him, enabled him to continue the slow rhythm of his breathing, the resting of his neck by the slow forward and backward bending, forward until his eyes were just above the surface, backward until his mouth was clear, forward… back… forward….

There was a chance, he instructed himself, that Barker and Nita together might affect a rescue. Barker was going to see Nita this morning, perhaps already was with her—Wentworth had no way of telling how long he had been unconscious. When the newspapers blazed forth the news that the Spider was held captive for El Gaucho, Barker would know where he was. Wentworth told himself that over and over again, but despair was in his breast and his thoughts did not erase its cold clamminess….

Backward… forward… backward… forward… Wentworth stiffened, his eyes widening. There, at the opposite end of the pool stood Yvonne Musette. She was smiling with that half-sullen lift of her red lips. She bent down, as Wentworth watched, to a brass disc in the tiling at her feet, opened it and reached inside. Instantly, Wentworth became aware of a bubbling of the water just at the surface below where she stood. Yvonne had turned on the water in the pool! Why, damn it, within minutes, it would cover his mouth, crawl toward his nostrils….

Yvonne straightened, smiling more merrily now than before.

Then she sauntered toward the end where his chair had been placed. "The water do not come in too fast," she explained, happily. "You will have time to t'ink of the reasons why I keel you, before you finally die...."

She bent close, spat into Wentworth's face.

"Have your good time, Yvonne," the Spider said gently. "The reckoning is coming." He breathed deeply, submerged to his eyes again, watched her with a calm confidence he had difficulty putting into his gaze.

Yvonne laughed and sauntered from the room, hips swaying, her whole body gesturing mockery... Wentworth gazed at that bubble of onrushing water at the other end. At most, he could not hold out longer than an hour. After that....

The Spider's jaw clenched until muscles bunched along the margin of his face. He closed his eyes. There was a faintness within him. He thought: *Death!* He thought: *This is the end!* He thought: *Nita...!*

CHAPTER 6
TO THE RESCUE!

DAWN HAD come and gone. The sun was high. Still sleepless, Nita van Sloan lounged on the silken cushions of the long, low seat before the huge studio window that looked out over the river traffic of the Hudson. Her eyes were unseeing. Two hours now since Dick Wentworth had phoned to say that he was beginning another attack. Two hours... and no further word.

She looked down at the slim whiteness of her hands, and her eyes were vacant, staring. During the night, those eyes had brimmed with tears, for it was in the silent, dark hours that the fears she never allowed Dick to see arose to smite down the intrepid courage that dwelt in her slim body; it was during the night that the frustration of their love harried her most. And then it was that she quivered with the fear of death... Dick Wentworth's death.

That was at night. With the sun something strange and fierce came into Nita van Sloan's soul. Dick had called briefly, and she had bade him be careful. Nita threw back her head, so that the sweet, long line of her throat was taut, and laughed. Dear God, let the Spider be careful! And now she was waiting, waiting. Always she must wait. She sprang to her feet and moved about the room, a slim, lovely girl in her full-cut lounging pajamas of maroon velvet. Her white hands moved restlessly, shifting a vase on the mantel above the fireplace, plumping a cushion in a chair.

Always she was anxious for Dick's safety, but this night there was a new depth to her terror. Dick had called uselessly. That meant he felt it, too; that he had wanted once more to hear her voice, perhaps for a last time... Nita hurled from her the pillow she was plumping, stood tautly facing the doorway of her home. Dick had assigned her a task to perform, to take care of Tom Barker, the grandson of dear old Professor Brownlee. But, good Lord, why didn't he come? She could do anything except wait....

It was half past eight when the doorbell rang. Calmness dropped upon Nita's tortured being like soothing oil. Her hand dropped to the pocket on her pajamas, touched lingeringly the stubby automatic that rested there. She thought it would be Tom Barker ringing, but the enemies of the Spider had struck at her before now. She went swiftly to the kitchen and allowed a massive Great Dane to bound out. He frisked like a puppy, tongue lolling out over cruel fangs.

Nita said, "Quiet, Apollo. On guard!"

The dog came to her side, great shoulder against her thigh, and she dropped her left hand to his big head. Together they moved toward the front door. She flicked aside the peephole cover.

Frank eyes under tousled hair looked into hers, a sun-tanned face, a smile that showed glistening teeth. Nita opened the door. The man—he was little more than a boy—held out a newspaper toward her, then let her see into the palm of his browned hand. A white card lay there, and on it—the seal of the Spider.

Nita swept open the door. "Back, Apollo," she ordered softly and took the boy into her gay studio room. The boy could not resist a wondering look about the place, the cool green linen that draped the big window; and Nita… He stared at her. If the vigil had shadowed her eyes, it had only deepened their violet hue. Her chestnut curls made a clustering frame for the perfect oval of her face. Her lips were… kind.

He shuffled his feet. "Morning, ma'am. I guess you know who I come from. Is Mr. Wentworth here?"

"No. Why do you ask?"

He pointed to the seal which he had given to Nita.

"*He* said Mr. Wentworth would help me, and you'd know what I was to do."

NITA STUDIED him carefully, and for a moment the boy lost his awareness of her beauty. Something that seemed suddenly grim and tight-lipped about her made him gaze with doubt and surprise. In a flash then, that impression was gone and again it was a gracious woman who motioned him to a chair.

"Sit down, won't you?" she said. "You're Tom Barker, of course. Mr. Wentworth is out of the city just now. What can I…?"

Tom Barker dropped into a chair, tossing the newspaper to a little table beside him. It spread open and black headlines shouted at Nita. Even the perfect control which the Spider's schooling had given her was not proof against what she saw. Those eyes widened and her words choked in her throat. She snatched the newspaper and there was a tremor in her bands that rustled the sheets.

She whispered, "Oh God! Oh, God!" The headlines swam before her eyes, tilted crazily, but that could not change their phrasing:

GANG CAPTURES SPIDER!
FAMOUS KILLER HOSTAGE FOR EL GAUCHO!
CRIMINALS' SPOKESMAN DECLARES
THAT NEW YORK UNDERWORLD
INVITES TERROR TO RULE IN EAST!

Nita's eyes went over the story. She forced them to, though she scarcely could grasp the import with her dazed mind.

She was aware of Barker saying something—

"What is it?" she asked.

"It's hell, ma'am. I was going to show it to Mr. Wentworth.

64

That Spider is a fine guy. Got me out of a jam...."

The words faded from Nita's mind. She drove the shocked incredulity from her heart and read, her face white, her eyes wide. The text of the Underworld's invitation to El Gaucho was there. The bandit leader of the West was assured of their ability and willingness to throw  New York City wide open to him; he would have all the loot he desired; the Spider was being held for some of his choicest tortures.

Another column told of the pursuit of El Gaucho after the last of his raids. Two automobiles loaded with police had crashed into a pit and set off a dynamite mine which had blown them to pieces. A man had been found dead, arms and legs torn from his body in some unimaginable way....

Nita crushed the papers in her hands, staring over Barker's head. "Damn them!" she said huskily. "Damn them! *They shall not!*"

Barker would not have known the voice for the rippling charming one he had heard a few moments before. Nita tossed the paper to the table as if it were unclean, leaving the boy to stare after her as she strode to a telephone, snarled Dick's number into the instrument. She must not let herself think of Dick, but only of smashing through to rescue him. Barker would know where to go.

"Ram Singh!" Her voice was sharp and imperative. "You and

Jackson come here at once. Buy a paper on the way. Yes, at once! Yes, Ram Singh, the *sahib!*"

Her face was set as she came back to confront Barker. "I'm going to the Spider's rescue," she said, her voice flat, incisive. "Mr. Wentworth, your grandfather's friend, is a close associate of the Spider, although the fact is not known. I am trusting you with that information so you will understand the necessity of telling me everything you know. You see if… Mr. Wentworth…. were here, he would go to the rescue of the Spider at once." Nita's voice faltered. It was as if the lie she told wrung her heart. *If Mr. Wentworth were here…* She made herself go on. "I have called two of Mr. Wentworth's men. You see? You understand? I want to know everything about where you left the Spider—all that he said and why and what, quickly… quickly…!"

Barker stared at her, swallowed. "You'll excuse me… those are mighty bad men. Tough eggs. It's no job for a lady. It…."

Something oddly like a shadow of the Spider's grim face touched the features of her lovely face.

"Talk!" ordered Nita van Sloan.

TOM BARKER talked, short explanations constantly interrupted by her incessant, "Yes, yes… and then?" Two other men entered. He noted subconsciously that they entered with their own keys. One stood on each side of the doorway, a lean, dour Hindu, his burning eyes straight before him, turbaned head held high. There was a tautness in all his powerful body, and there was a curved knife at his belt.

The other was a wide-shouldered man who bore himself with military erectness. His face was square, the jaws wide and knotted with muscles. There was a grimness in both their faces. Nita's head pulled about toward the latter man.

"You read the papers, Jackson?"

"Yes, Miss Nita," Jackson's voice was clipped, had a hard ring. "I read them to Ram Singh, too. What are the orders?"

"A machine gun, Jackson. Three drums of ammunition. Two automatics around." Nita's voice was as clipped and sharp as his own. There was a lift to it now, an urgency. "Fix thirty-eights for me. I can handle them a little better."

Jackson snapped a salute. "You know anything about the major, ma'am?" Jackson had been Wentworth's sergeant during the war. He still preferred to use the service titles.

Nita said flatly, "I only know what I read in the papers. Barker, on with the story."

"That's about all, ma'am," Barker said slowly, watching the two grim-faced men through a curtained door across the room.

"The Spider left me. I don't think there's any doubt about where he was going. I don't know whether they kept him there or not...."

Nita nodded, went out through another doorway and returned in an incredibly short time dressed in a dark, close-fitting suit, a tight hat over her eyes. Ram Singh and Jackson came back. Jackson carried over his arm a lap-robe that bulged strangely.

"Orders, Miss Nita?" Jackson's blue eyes were hard and sharp on Nita's, but it was obvious from his manner that he was devoted to her—that he would follow her orders to the death. The muscles kept working along the bulge of his wide jaws.

"I'll give them on the way," Nita said crisply. "Ram Singh, take us to Forty-fifth and Sixth Avenue."

Ram Singh flashed his white teeth in a smile, bowing, sweeping cupped hands to his forehead in a salaam.

"Han, missie sahib!" His hand dropped to the knife at his side. "We fight then?"

"We fight!"

"Say, I want to be in on this," Barker exclaimed.

Nita nodded. "You are in!"

It was a silent company that trooped to the car, a heavy low-swung sedan with a motor that throbbed with power. Once under way Nita spoke concisely, telling them what Barker had said in half the number of words.

"As soon as we enter the building—Ram Singh and Barker and I—Jackson, I want you to drive the car to a point near the entrance, wait there five minutes with the machine gun, then come in. I don't think there's much doubt we will be ambushed. You're to shoot us out of it."

Jackson's lips slitted in a grin. "Yes, Miss Nita."

Nita turned to Barker. "Can you use a revolver or automatic?" she asked quietly.

Barker nodded eagerly. "Either one, ma'am. I used to be a pretty good shot."

Nita reached into a compartment of the car and drew out a thirty-eight revolver. Barker took it, handled it expertly with its muzzle pointed downward. Then, looking at her, he shoved it in his coat pocket.

"Not going to call the police?"

Nita smiled slightly. "I don't think that would be a good idea."
SHE SAT looking straight before her then while the car was tooled expertly through traffic. It was still a little early for the automobile traffic rush, though subways would be jammed. The building she planned to attack, too, would be nearly deserted. Elevator operators would be working, of course. A few early arrivals… Nita's mind turned from the battle ahead to Dick. He would count on some such raid, certainly, for he knew that Barker was coming to her and that she would glean all his information. If he could, he would smash through to help….

Nita's eyes felt dry and feverish. Her hand strayed to her purse, to her coat pocket. Both her light guns were ready. There was a tension throughout her body: a slight, tight smile on her lips. They would win through because they *must*….

Barker's voice broke into her thoughts. "Look here, ma'am. I've got a scheme. They know me and think I'm with them. Let me go ahead. I'll find out where the Spider is and then…."

Nita asked gently, "And then what?"

Barker looked downcast. "You don't reckon they'd let me get out again?"

Nita shook her head, but there was another thought in her mind. She was as inclined to trust this boy as Dick was. He had come to her alone, without gangster trailers apparently. But there was always a chance that he was playing some obscure game. God knew there had been enough treachery… Ram Singh drew the car to a halt, sprang to the pavement and Jackson took his place behind the wheel. Nita's doubts and fears left her. Her hands went once more to her hidden guns.

"Five minutes, Jackson," she commanded softly.

Jackson grinned at her. "I'll shave that, ma'am, if I hear shooting?"

Nita nodded and walked up the street, Barker beside her, Ram Singh just behind, walking with the long, free swing of the mountain Sikhs from whom he sprang, his eyes intent, teeth just showing between his lips. His hand strayed ever and again to the knife at his girdle. There were two other knives hidden under his tunic that he used for throwing and the knife at his side he never drew except to shed human blood. It was curved and its inner edge was razor-sharp. A stroke would disembowel a man neatly....

The doors of the building were wide, hooked back to the walls. Two men lounged about the foyer within, talking idly to the elevator starter. When Nita and Barker walked in, they looked about quickly, then turned back to their conversation. Nita's hand gestured behind her and Ram Singh fell back, halting just outside the outer doorway, while Nita and Barker walked straight toward the stairway that led downward.

The starter called, "Who did you want, madam? That's a men's club down there."

Nita ignored him and Barker fell in behind her as she went downward. Nita felt him hesitate when he saw the two men who had been talking with the starter move in their direction, heads lowered a little, hands rising to underarm guns.

"Ram Singh will take care of them," Nita told Barker.

The stair descended along three sides of a square, three short flights downward. When Nita reached the middle of the second flight, the two men above began to move downward, too. As soon as they were out of sight of the foyer, their guns snapped into their hands.

"Just wait there, baby!" one of them called gruffly.

NITA TURNED a cold, set face toward them, saw Ram Singh come softly around the corner. His knife was not in his hand. He would not draw except to kill, but that knife could leap into action as quickly as a man could squeeze a trigger. Nita waited and Ram Singh came softly, swiftly downward.

One of the men whirled about abruptly when Ram Singh was two steps above him. A startled cry burst from his throat and he threw up his gun. He would have done better to drop it and cry for mercy. As his weapon nosed up, Ram Singh's arm crossed his body. The knife flashed from its sheath, speared forward. With a gurgling, startled cry, the gunman collapsed. Ram Singh, standing high, had been forced to strike for the throat. But even as he stabbed, he sprang forward, and the second gunman, whirling to face this unsuspected danger, caught the knife in his belly.

The starter was at the head of the steps now, staring down upon the white steps that were now smeared with crimson. Nita presented an automatic. "Come down here!" she called sharply.

Nita's eyes avoided the dead men on the stairs. Nausea was tugging at her stomach, and she felt a faintness sweep toward her brain. But she did not waver on her feet. The gun in her hand was steady. The elevator starter trembled. Ram Singh started toward him, the red knife in his hand, and the man turned and ran, screaming. Nita did not fire. She looked down at the gun in her hand.

"He hadn't done anything," she murmured dully. "I couldn't shoot him."

Barker thrust her sharply on the shoulder and below them, from the basement, a gun barked twice thunderously. Nita dropped to her knee on the step and Barker crouched behind the marble railing. Ram Singh's right arm swept down and a streak of glinting, steely light flashed down the stairs. From behind the corner of the wall at the foot of the steps, a man staggered into view, both hands plucking at his throat from which the brass-bound hilt of a knife protruded. His knees caved and he slammed hard on his face.

Ram Singh came down the stairs softly, lifting Nita to her feet with one brawny hand. His stabbing knife was back in its scabbard. In his left hand, he held a second straight-bladed throwing knife.

"*Wah! Missie sahib,*" his harsh, nasal voice rasped. "These are not warriors whom we fight. They are...."

The ripping batter of machine-gun bullets, slashing down from behind, choked his voice in his throat. He blundered down the steps, falling. Nita's gun spat this time and up there, where two men already had died, another slumped down, his weapon stilled. Nita's paleness now was not the pallor of faintness but of anger. She crouched beside Ram Singh, who was striving valiantly to drag his wounded body up from the platform where he had fallen. There was a running red stain on his back.

"*Wah! Missie sahib,*" he whispered. "It is nothing, nothing at all! In a moment..." Ram Singh slumped down unconscious on the stairs. There were more guns above now, spatting bullets.

Nita heard Barker's gun spit and she opened up with a slow, deliberate fire. For all that, lead began to whistle uncomfortably close, to snick flecks of plaster from the walls.

"You run, ma'am," whispered Barker. "I'll hold them."

Nita snapped a shot at a gun hand that showed itself over the marble railing above, saw that hand stiffen bloodily and withdraw. She whispered back. "You're forgetting Jackson."

For a dozen breaths, there was silence above, then a thunderous splash of sound washed through the hallway, revolvers spitting and the heavier, overwhelming chatter of a machine gun.

Nita's eyes were agate hard. One hand was on Ram Singh's shoulder; the other was clasping her automatic. She patted the Hindu's shoulder; then she sprang erect, went down the stairs swiftly.

"That's Jackson," she said. "Come on, Barker."

IT WOULD have to be swift and deadly now, or the police would crash into the battle, and all would be lost, even if they had rescued Wentworth by then. She pounded down the steps, whirled the corner of the hall where a man lay dead with Ram Singh's knife in his throat. She sprang clear of the wall and instantly her automatic began to speak. Four men were coming down the hall in a bunch, three with automatics, the fourth with a machine gun. One of them staggered and fell from the impact of Nita's lead.

A bullet burned Nita's throat and she threw herself down on her face, still firing. A second man sat down suddenly on the floor, arms doubled over his belly. But the machine gun was being lifted now, the man's face behind it was debonair, smiling beneath a smooth, black cap of hair. He was well over six feet, and there was enjoyment in his every gesture.

Barker suddenly threw down his gun and raced toward the man. "Don't shoot, Peterson! Don't shoot, I'm with you!"

He was directly in front of the machine gun now, between Nita and that deadly muzzle.

Nita lifted her automatic deliberately, her lips drawing back from her teeth. The coward, the dirty traitor! Barker's friendliness had all been trickery. In the instant she lifted her weapon to shoot him down, Barker was hurled aside by one of the gunmen. Nita sprang to her feet, firing quick shots, and before the machine gun could target on her again, she flung herself across the hall, took cover behind the corner of the steps. Jackson was on the platform above her.

"What's up, Miss Nita?" he whispered. "Ram Singh's bad hit."

"Barker turned traitor," Nita snapped. "Turn your machine gun around that corner and…."

A hammering hail of bullets clawed the edge off the corner, sent lead ricocheting up the marble balustrade, chipping the steps. Nita shrank back from it, reloading her automatic rapidly. There was blazing anger in her mind and despair in her soul. How could they fight their way through that leaden rain before police came? It would do no good for Jackson to attempt an attack around that corner. He would be sieved with lead….

Jackson caught Nita by the shoulder, dragged her up to where he stood with the machine gun braced at ready.

"Ram Singh can walk if you brace him, Miss Nita," he said sharply. "Better help him up the stairs."

Nita stood crouched behind Jackson with her gun ready. The lead continued to splat about the corner, to whine off the balustrade. She heard what Jackson said, but the words didn't register in her brain. There was only one thought in her brain, could be only one. To get down those steps and reach Dick, snatch him from this trap.

"Quickly, Miss Nita," Jackson's voice rang out. "Get Ram Singh out of this!"

Nita said, "No, no!" It was under her breath, scarcely audible. She repeated it again, "No, no. We must save Dick. *We must!*"

Jackson's gun hammered and Nita saw the muzzle of a machine gun beaten back from the corner of the wall. It spat a few bullets but they went wide.

"For God's sake, Miss Nita," Jackson said hoarsely. "You know I wouldn't desert the major if there was a chance. Retreat and we'll try again. There are only two of us now…" The chatter of his gun drowned his words and even above it came the high weird whine of police sirens.

NITA STAGGERED up the steps. Bullets sang about her, but she did not notice them. Her mind was blank. They had tried to save Dick and failed. She stooped above Ram Singh, put a hand under his arm, dragged it across her shoulders. The Hindu fought his way to his feet, leaning heavily upon Nita.

"We… retreat?"

"We retreat," Nita mumbled dully. She saw Jackson backing toward them swiftly, the machine gun before him. Once more that vicious snout poked around the corner of the wall and once more Jackson hammered it with bullets. Nita felt lead pluck at her skirt, but scarcely heeded. Why, good God, they were leaving Dick back there, leaving him to be murdered! She stopped on the stairway and Ram Singh reeled, braced a great hand against the wall.

"It is… wise, *missie sahib,*" he gasped. "This way we live… to fight again!"

Nita was dully aware of screams above her in the hallway, of the louder shrilling of the police sirens. Nita heard Jackson curse.

"Down!" he shouted. "My gun's empty!"

Nita turned stiffly to stare down the stairway, saw Jackson crouched to fit in another drum of ammunition. Down below, the tall, smiling man whom Barker had called Peterson leaped clear with the machine gun's muzzle lifted toward them. Nita snatched up her automatic and fired with the same motion. It was instinctive—a reflex of her body, for her brain was stupid with grief.

Down in the basement, Peterson reeled backward against the wall, a bloody smear across his temple. The machine gun dropped from his arms, and he rolled along the wall, his hands groping, then flopped down on his face. Jackson sprang up the stairs, threw a powerful arm about Ram Singh and they went swiftly up to the foyer. Jackson fired a short burst into the ceiling and men who clustered there fearfully turned and fled. Women screamed shrilly. Jackson released his hold on Ram Singh and ran for the door.

Moments later, the giant Daimler, mighty engine humming, was at the door. Ram Singh pulled himself free, flung into the front seat while Nita sprang into the rear.

The car leaped forward. Blazed through traffic... vanished.

Back at the scene of battle, two men came sedately upstairs from the athletic club to meet the police. They said all they knew was that some people had started firing when they tried to come up the stairs. No, they didn't know those people. All that plaster and the holes? They really didn't know. The police sergeant looked glumly at the evidence of considerable shooting and walked through what he believed to be the entire club establishment and went out.

"Lay off," he growled to an earnest young policeman who continued to buzz the bystanders. "Lay off! Don't cha know who owns this club?"

"What of it?" indignantly demanded the rookie policeman.

The sergeant flipped a weary hand at him. "On your way." He extended the gesture to the gathering crowd. "G'wan. Nothin' happened. Just a coupla friends playing tag, see? On your way!"

In the Daimler, purring smoothly down Riverside Drive, a wild-eyed young woman stared straight before her.

"I'll kill him," she said flatly. "The next time I see him, I'll kill him. The traitor! To think that he would desert to the enemies of the Spider...."

Jackson kept his eyes straight ahead, but there was a grim, hard set to his broad shoulders. Ram Singh leaned back weakly against the cushions. There was a doctor friend of Wentworth's who would care for his wounds....

Nita's head sagged forward. She lifted her hands to her face. She had failed, failed. She was Dick's only hope and she had failed him… After a while, her shoulders began to jerk in rhythm with her sobbing.…

CHAPTER 7
THE TRAITOR

I T WAS very quiet in the room of the pool. There was only the soft whisper of the water to be heard. In that room, two pairs of steady, heavy-lidded eyes stared fixedly into each other. One pair of eyes belonged to a man and was just above the waterline in the pool. The man's head tilted back at regular intervals of a half minute, so that the nose and the mouth were clear for the space of two breaths. Then the face sank until water crossed the bridge of the nose. The eyes never ceased to hold the other's.

The other eyes were those of a too sleek, too lithe, woman. She stood at the foot of the pool. In her hand there was a gun, held as steadily as though it rested on a support. The man in the water was so near exhaustion that only the exercise of the supernatural will, that was the Spider's strength, held him from sinking to his death. Flashes of red flickered before his eyes, and a wave of black oblivion rose again and again. He fought it back doggedly.

Nita! It was that one word which brought up Wentworth's head against the shrieks of tortured nerves and lungs and muscles. But at the back of his mind a giant hammer seemed to beat constantly with *"finished—finished—finished"* as its refrain. Hours of this slow lift and bowing of his head that must not cease.

Yvonne gloated at his discomfort. "You keel my Oscaire. I shoot you for that. You keel Tom Barkaire—I kill you again for that. I lofe my Oscaire and I could lofe that Tom Barkaire. Now that police come 'ere I mus' keel you wit' the gun instead of wait for the so nice water to do it for me...."

She leveled the gun. The Spider's eyes never wavered. *Here it comes, that thing you have escaped so often, now, at last,* said that hammering in his head, and something monstrous and chill flooded all of his body. He felt it as a thing alive, as a cold breath from another world invading his vitals. As in the gaze of all men about to die, and knowing it, there came a terrible power, a ghastly, weird beauty of unblinking, fixed, enlarged eyes. Many a murderer has been at least momentarily halted by such eyes of a victim. Even the hardened woman felt an instant's shock. It stayed her hand.

At that moment, someone began tapping along the wall of the room, the wall that showed no doorway anywhere. Yvonne's eyes turned toward the sound and the Spider, desperately braced against the unconsciousness which would long since have struck down any lesser man, almost slipped into the blackness through sheer relief from the pressure of her cruel, mocking eyes.

Beyond the wall, a voice began calling, a voice the Spider could not rouse himself to answer:

"Spider—Spider—it's Barker! Spider, *can you hear me?* It's Tom!"

Yvonne gave a strangled cry, ran to open a secret sliding door. She met the man with uplifted arms. The Spider saw the gun clasped between the shoulders of Tom Barker as her arms went about his neck.

"Honey bunch," Barker half-laughed, "you sure got sudden ways. Glad to see me, huh?"

"I thought *he* keel you. Where you been?"

"Oh, around. What's happened here, girlie? The boys blow out and leave you holding the fort?"

"The poleece—but first, some othairs—very much shooting. It was better I keel this Spider."

"I SEE." Barker walked over and looked down at the Spider. The Spider tilted back his head and looked up, breathing gaspingly. He clung to the remnants of his consciousness. Friend or foe, this Tom Barker? Wentworth did not know. The water whispered softly. He realized that in a few minutes more it would be impossible, even with his steely will, to keep his nose out of it. It was already impossible to lift his mouth above its level. Barker looked down, speculatively, seemingly without a trace of interest.

"Going to shoot him, eh?" he mused. "El Gaucho will be nice and pleased, I don't think, to have it spread all over the papers that he has the redoubtable Spider here waiting for him and then, when he comes, find that someone bumped off his special game for him."

"I don't care. I keel him. He keel my Oscaire."

"Here, here," Barker bantered, "I thought it was *me* that you had a crush on."

Yvonne's face had hardened and she moved away from Barker to the end of the pool which faced the Spider. Barker said seriously: "Listen here, baby, you'll get yourself in an awful mess doing that."

He sidled cautiously toward her, and realized suddenly that a small door immediately behind her had opened. He pointed to it then sprang to throw his big arms about her. She shot but her aim was wild and she turned, spitting like a wild cat, only to have the soft-spoken Peterson, a bloody smear across his forehead, smile maddeningly at her. It was he who had slipped through the door. Barker gave Yvonne to Peterson's long, powerful arms.

"Just what do you think you are up to, my darling?" laughed Peterson. "Going to take away one of our best reasons for getting in touch with El Gaucho? You will have to be disciplined, little devil." He looked at Barker. "Thanks for coming to my aid out there in the hall. That dame of the Spider's had a bead on my head and she'd have dropped me cold meat if you hadn't butted in."

The Spider's eyes shot open and he made another exhausted effort to keep from sinking beneath the water. *Nita*—he had not even heard the shooting. But now he knew. She had come to rescue him and been driven back. Now his last hope was gone. He felt muscles relaxing throughout his body. That dread blackness was very near....

As if the Spider had spoken, Peterson turned to him, still holding the squirming Yvonne easily, as though she were a rag doll. "Yes, Spider, that girl of yours came with two men. They made Barker show them the place, but just as soon as he could he let me know he was with us. Some piece of fire, that lady— but all nice girls are like that." He smiled down at the raging

PETERSON

YVONNE

BARKER

Yvonne, then suddenly threw her from him on the slack of his arms, so that she slammed against the wall, gasped, and slumped to the floor unconscious. Not by the flick of an eyelid did Peterson show awareness of her.

Now there were other men in the room, but the Spider, his ears full of water, the hammering in his ears a vast, cosmic clash of doom, was too near death to heed or care. Nita had been driven back. All hope was gone. This was… the end….

"If you want to save the Spider for El Gaucho," said Barker, coolly, "you'd better haul him out. Unless I'm mistaken, he'll be gone in another minute or two."

EVEN AS Barker spoke, the

blackness triumphed at last. It rushed over Wentworth with a clap like a thunderous wave. His head sagged forward beneath the water so that only a scalp lock of black hair was awash on the surface.

Barker cried, "Hey! Wait!" He jumped into the water and lifted the Spider's face above the surface. "You want him alive, Peterson?"

Peterson was scowling. "Hell, no, I don't *want* him. But I got to have him for the Gaucho. Hold on, feller, and…."

"Get in there, Scottie, and give him a hand."

They got the Spider loose finally and laid him out on the tiles. Barker left him then, wringing water out

EL GAUCHO

CAROLLOTTA

VON HAPSZOLLERN

of his coattails, out of the cuffs of his trousers. Peterson came around and grinned down while the man called Scottie poured whiskey down Wentworth's throat, slapped his cheeks to restore circulation.

"Listen, Peterson," Barker said, "if you don't mind my saying so, we got to do some tall moving out of here. That bunch of flatfeet that was here a while ago may get frozen dogs because they're afraid of you big noises, but there's others, higher up, that will come around."

"You are all fools." Yvonne had staggered to her feet and stood, glowering. "You will regret that you make me angree!"

"Yes, darling," Peterson agreed. His face was bland but Yvonne shrank, turned pale and said nothing more. Barker laughed, and sauntered over to put an arm caressingly about her shoulders, whispered in her ear. A reluctant, vanity-stirred smile crept over Yvonne's mouth.

The Spider regained consciousness with the taste of whiskey on his lips. He rolled his heavy eyelids up and saw the smiling face of Peterson bending over him.

"That's good, men," Peterson purred. "Got to get you up and out, m'lad. The cops will be here—some of the higher-ups are trampling over the bodies of our friends on the Force. Come on now, shake a leg—" The hands which heaved the Spider to his feet were strong and cruel. They shut down like pincers on the arms. A man in less superb condition than the Spider and so recently near death would have fainted at the pain. But although Peterson looked sideways under his cruel eyelids, he could not see even a quiver on the strange face of the man who already was beginning to walk almost firmly. The miracle of that recovery was so great that even the hardened men who ringed him around looked with half-superstitious awe at the Spider. Some of the fear with which his name had always been associated came over them. They threw his clothes upon him, fell back and left him to walk alone. His long black cape clung to him like a shroud; he was the color of putty—but, somehow, inexpressibly terrible. His hands were bound tightly and the wrists swollen, he staggered as he walked, but hope and fierce rage sprang up in him.

His escape *was* a miracle. Belief in his mission, in the power of fate, flailing a great, protective sword above his head, made him radiate a confidence, a power which could actually be felt. Men fell back before him. But when he passed through the little, secret door at the back of the room, he would have fallen down the steps if Barker had not caught him....

IT WAS as the young man caught his elbow that the Spider was galvanized by a flash of hope, for those fingers pressed in a strange series of nips, holds and repeated pressures, rhythmic as breathing. It couldn't be, but... it was! *Morse code!* Barker was trying to give him some message!

Stairs went down steeply into a cellar. "Go ahead of me," Barker said impatiently, to the rest of them. "This guy can't walk easy and I'm damned if I'll carry him. He might throttle me."

The men all crowded past and again the fingers started their silent talk on Wentworth's arm. *I had to play it this way; Peterson had the lady covered*—The Spider's preternaturally keen senses were dulled. He found it hard to follow the unaccustomed signaling, but he got it finally and the hope that had burgeoned within him grew stronger. If one were on his side, he could achieve miracles. He used his elbow to press out a laborious message.

"Where are we going?"

He glanced sideways out of his eyes, saw Barker shaking his head. Well, it did not matter. With an ally in camp, he could conquer. Just now he needed rest… rest…. They left the building by way of a dark alley and entered two powerful cars. Wentworth relaxed and slept.

HE AWOKE to find the cars rolling into Newark airport. He looked around. Peterson, seated beside him, was climbing out as an official strode to meet him. The gangster made no attempt to hide the gun in his hand; guns were in the other men's hands, too, and Wentworth peered about, saw that several more sedans had mysteriously fallen in behind them.

"Plane chartered by phone an hour ago," Peterson rasped. "Name? Does that matter? Conduct us to it and I'd like to have about two more."

The official, white as his collar, stuttered, "Th—th—there isn't—aren't—any others!"

"Oh, yes, there are," said Peterson, gently, "and if there are not, it will be extremely unfortunate for a number of people—not in my party, my dear fellow."

THE FRIGHTENED eyes of the airport agent, uncertainly standing beside the car, fell on the Spider, his hands now held in handcuffs. "You—you are officers?" the man stuttered. "Is—are you demanding these planes in the name of the law—for a prisoner?"

Peterson laughed gently. "For a prisoner, yes—for the law? Oh, no! For the outlaws!"

The Spider smiled bleakly. Peterson was enjoying himself and, since he had spoken, Wentworth was no longer interested in escape. Not for the present, at least. The sense of power was in his veins again. No doubt now as to the destination of Peterson and his gang. They flew to a rendezvous with El Gaucho! It was well. The Spider would rest and gather strength for the battle to come....

A small cabin plane taxied up, the white, startled face of the pilot peering from the cockpit. One of the gang stood over him,

a gun at the aviator's head. Barker and the Spider, Peterson and Scottie got in. The plane lumbered down the field, turned into the wind, got under way. Wentworth peered down at the field as it dropped away. The bitter, sardonic spirit of the Spider, which had held him until that moment, went away and Wentworth— who loved the sweetest woman in the world, and was neither sardonic nor bitter—thought strangely that it was as if he were really dead and were leaving Wentworth behind.

Barker seemed entirely indifferent toward the Spider, although he sat near him and whistled tonelessly. The heavy drone of the motors beat upon Wentworth's brain, numbing his exhausted sensibilities. He leaned his head back and slept.... He had no idea how much time had passed when a touch on his elbow awakened him. He looked about cautiously. Barker still gazed out of the window and whistled without tune. Peterson, ahead, dozed over a newspaper and, across the aisle, the man called Scottie, sandy-gray head bowed on his chest, was sleeping, too.

Barker looked toward Wentworth and, still whistling, bent as if to tie his shoelace and with a pocket knife he had palmed, sliced through the bonds about Wentworth's ankles. The Spider almost cried out for him to cease, that he did not wish to escape yet. They were headed for the spot where they would meet El Gaucho... then his eyes became crafty. It would be better to be free to act then, and he had a plan....

Barker reached across the aisle then, slipped a small key into the handcuffs on Wentworth's wrists and tried to turn it.

It rasped, made a snapping sound and—

"Put 'em up, boys," said Scottie, lifting the head that had seemed to sleep. Wentworth's gaze jerked that way and he looked into the black eye of a leveled gun. "Damn it, put 'em up. Didn't I tell you, Peterson? I told you this guy was a double-crosser." The gun was steady, the man's evil squinting face alight. "Shall I bump 'em?"

"By no means, my dear chap," Peterson murmured. "Have we brought them thus far to surrender live hostages to the Gaucho only to—er... a—bump them off now? Not at all, my dear Scottie. It's just...."

Wentworth flashed a warning glance at Barker and sprang toward Scottie with his manacles jerked high. He saw Barker's hand dive for his gun pocket and then he had closed with Scottie. The man threw his left arm high as a shield and leveled the  revolver beneath it, but he had not calculated on the violence of the Spider's blow. When the handcuffs slashed down against his left elbow, the arm went limp and a howl of pain tore from Scottie's lips. He dropped the gun and grabbed for his elbow. His lower arm swung limply, the bone fractured.

Wentworth heard a shot behind him, heard Barker groan. Peterson, laughing, was still in his seat with an automatic resting on his knee.

"My dear Barker, did you really think I would give you a loaded gun?" he asked gently.

Barker was sagging back into his chair, grasping his shoulder, and Peterson's gun was turned now toward Wentworth.

"I have no intention of killing you, Spider," said Peterson, "but I can break a leg or an arm…."

The flat, mocking laughter of the Spider filled the cabin, cutting through the roar of the motor. Scottie had shrunk away from Wentworth's attack, moaning over his arm. Wentworth caught him by coat lapels and whipped him about, hurled him almost bodily toward where Peterson sat. He went charging in behind Scottie.

The plane slithered and jerked under Wentworth's feet and

he saw the white, frightened face of the pilot show in the doorway. The Spider laughed again. Strength was leaping through his veins. Once more he raised his handcuffs and slashed down with them. Scottie groaned and pitched to the floor, and Wentworth sprang forward with his manacles lifted....

As Scottie fell, Peterson's legs came up and Wentworth fought vainly to dodge the two-footed kick that lanced straight for his chest. He staggered backward with the violence of that blow, tangled with Barker who was rising to resume the battle. The two of them tangled on the floor.

"For God's sake!" the pilot screamed. "You'll wreck us."

Peterson's fast breathing interfered with his laughter, but he laughed hoarsely anyway. He ran his left hand through his black hair to smooth it into place, held his gun ready.

"Listen," he said raspingly, "I don't want to kill you two, but I by God will if you move again."

He squeezed the trigger of his automatic and a bullet smacked into a seat within an inch of Wentworth's head. He gazed up into Peterson's face and realized that the man meant precisely what he said. The murder light was in Peterson's small, black eyes. Scottie was slouching to his knees, staggering to his feet. He turned about with his broken arm swinging, stepped close and slammed his good fist into Wentworth's face. The Spider had only time to set his jaw and tense his neck muscles. Long ago he had learned that trick in the prize ring to prevent a knockout. Scottie turned and hit Barker viciously, then the two gangsters went cautiously about binding their prisoners to the seats.

Wentworth felt his weariness swarm over him again, felt the cold hint of despair. He fought it down and smiled slowly, the harsh, mocking smile of the Spider.

"A nice little party, wasn't it?" he said softly.

Scottie slugged him again....

CHAPTER 8
AUDIENCE WITH EL GAUCHO!

IT WAS not a half hour later that the drone of the plane's engine dwindled and Wentworth felt the ship sag toward earth. He leaned toward the window, as did all others. The plane was settling down on a hard-packed field without hangars or other evidence of airship facilities. Beyond it, among a fringe of straggling trees, a few houses were scattered among streets of tents. The pilot bumped down and sat still, peering back with frightened eyes.

A big car with a strangely steady motion rolled out from the clump of trees and raced across the rough ground with surprising speed and ease, and with a curious straddling action of the wheels. The Spider had time as he climbed to the earth for a quick estimate that it was specially constructed for rough country. The auto halted and a military man in spotless but unfamiliar uniform of dark red got out, escorted by two orderlies in similar, plainer garb, who stood rigidly at attention behind him.

The officer's stern eye swept over the plane. He ignored Peterson and the other three, addressed the pilot who was climbing down from the ship.

"Pilot, have you fuel enough for a return trip?"

"Yes, sir," said the pilot, his deference enthusiastic as he realized the intention behind the man's question.

"Then you have our leave to go—at once!"

"Yes, *sir!*" The pilot sprang back to his ship, but Peterson's shout stopped him.

"You will remain here until I dismiss you. As for you," he turned to the officer, "we've come here to see El Gaucho—"

The orderlies behind the officer blew, simultaneously, two small silver whistles which were surprisingly shrill and clear. Instantly, some twenty men, all clad in the same dark uniforms and armed with machine guns, started at a trot toward the field. Wentworth smiled slightly as he saw the color drain from Peterson's face. The officer was scowling darkly, but if he planned to say anything it was drowned in the roar of the plane's motor as the pilot gunned and kicked the rudder to turn into the wind. A cloud of dust swept over them. The officer, whose black mustaches curved upward in brisk militant points, threw up an arm. The whistles piped again and the machine gunners halted, returned again to the trees.

Wentworth saw that they were well disciplined, well drilled and there was a speculative frown about his eyes as he gazed again at the brisk, mustached officer. What manner of criminal was this Gaucho that he had well-trained soldiers to serve him? The Spider shook his head. It was no wonder that he took cities with such ease. What chance did small-town police stand against disciplined troops? Wentworth's lips tightened against his teeth. Well, he would see how the troops would function without their leaders after the Spider struck!… He became aware that Peterson was answering the officer's questions, his debonair manner blanketed by sullenness.

"There will be two other planes here in a short while," Peterson growled. "D'you realize we have come here on an *official* visit to El Gaucho—on an important official visit—and that we are representing very important interests? We've brought the Spider, a captive."

The officer was utterly cold. "Learn to address yourself in better terms to your superiors, my man," he said, incisively. "I am not at all sure you will be permitted to see El Gaucho. If our Commander decides against it we will return you in our own plane. I will ask for an audience for you. If it is granted, you will remember not to speak unless you are spoken to. El Gaucho is one of the few authentic kings of an ancient line and of an ancient kingdom. Time only is needed to make him practically the sole ruler of the world!"

WENTWORTH WATCHED the man's face narrowly while he spoke. There was first contempt for Peterson and later when he spoke of El Gaucho, an exaltation. The Spider realized that the officer, at least, believed what he said. To him, El Gaucho was a king, a future world-ruler. And he had mentioned planes. Truly, the army was well equipped!

The officer turned his back, stalked away to his car alone; the orderlies remained to conduct the four new arrivals across the dusty field toward the trees. The sun beat down hotly. Wentworth, looking about at the well-armed, well-trained men, felt the slow rise of despair in his heart.

93

The men began to coax the horses forward; the ropes tightened!

Suddenly it seemed ridiculous that he, a lone man—and a prisoner at that!—should consider the possibility of victory over El Gaucho and his organization. They were all silent as they trudged across the sun-parched field. When automobiles bore them away, a few minutes later, the officer stayed behind, apparently waiting for the other planes.

It had not escaped the keen eyes of the Spider that while the land seemed flat for miles around, there really were depressions in it here and there. The cars followed a faint track in the heavy dust, the ground gradually rose, became rocky, began to run through scraggly trees into thicker timber. Abruptly it wound around a bend, and an exclamation of surprise came even from Peterson.

A sunken plateau lay below this mounting land, a mile wide, ringed about with rocky slopes, closed at the north to a narrow pass, opening out to the south. It had suffered less than most of the country in the dust storms which had ravaged the region, and there were patches of meadow and a fair-sized stream. Horses and cattle were grazing and there were some standing crops. At the widest part of the plateau, however, there were military arrangements. The wall of a fort, an immense parade ground, and streets of tents. In the rear, set in a ribbon of bright garden, formally laid out, was a small but very handsome house with a large pennant—a purple stripe above a bright scarlet one—flying on its flagstaff. Wentworth saw these things with a sense of amazement. Counting the tents, he estimated that there were enough for a thousand men!

He noticed many of them lolling about in front of the tents as the cars with the orderlies, Peterson, Barker, Scottie, and himself drew near. Wentworth and Barker were herded into a tent with the gangsters, and there they were kept under armed guard until the low sun sent golden shafts slanting through the tent flap and measured steps sounded outside. The guards stood, their guns snapping to present arms. The officer who had first received them at the air field stepped in and looked them over slowly with a dull, flat eye. He saw that Wentworth's wrists were still manacled and shortly demanded the key. Peterson surrendered it with a shrug.

"After all," he smiled blandly at the Spider, "you are now El Gaucho's prisoner, not mine. I hope that you enjoy your meeting."

THE OFFICER watched without expression as Barker was cut loose from the ropes that bound him. Wentworth stretched and massaged his wrists, eyes covertly surveying the tent. By a quick dash, he might spring behind his cot, roll out under the canvas wall… and then? But there would be a score of guards posted about with rifles. No, no, such a break required the sheltering kindness of night. He was in the midst of an armed camp. He crossed to Barker, threw an arm about the boy's shoulders.

"How you feel, Barker?"

Barker grinned up at him, white teeth flashing from his brown face. "Swelegant, Spider. Simply swelegant!"

Wentworth knew that the officer's eyes were upon him, but he ignored that, chatting lightly with the boy who had risked his life to help him. Still Wentworth managed to see Peterson's mocking grin, his wink toward the officer.

"Guess you know what you're doing, Chief," Peterson drawled, "but this Spider has the keenest reputation in the world for getting himself out of tight scrapes."

The officer ignored Peterson, but when the gangsters filed out of the tent, the two rifle-armed guards took a position on either side of Wentworth. An amused gleam touched the Spider's eyes. Rifles were splendid if a man were running from you, but when he was close…. Still nothing was to be gained by downing these two men and overpowering the officer. He could glimpse the uniformed legs of guards outside, forming a square about the gangsters. He looked directly into the officer's eyes.

The man nodded. "I am quite aware that you could make a break for it," he said, his manner much more courteous than that he used toward Peterson. "Your reputation has reached even to my country. But it would not be wise. There are too many rifles outside. It is possible the King will be… amiably… inclined toward you."

Wentworth bowed wordlessly, his gesture graceful despite the false hunch of his shoulders. Barker was looking at him admiringly, and there was no mistaking the respect in the officer's glance. He snapped a command at the two guards and, between them, Wentworth and Barker marched out through the tent flap, pivoted left. There were eight more soldiers waiting there and, at an order, they fell in before and in back of the two prisoners.

The Spider's eyes took in the entire scene, even the circling airplanes overhead which obviously kept watch over the field. Along the left side of the parade grounds, fronted by the tents, two companies of the red-clad soldiers were drawn up in faultless array. On the ends of the field, behind the troops, were a motley assembly of others who numbered fully a thousand. Mexicans in silver-slashed velvet and broad-brimmed sombreros; hard-bitten men of the plains with six-shooters strapped low on thighs; city-clothed men who obviously were gangsters as vicious as any Peterson might command.

These things were taken in at a glance, then Wentworth's eyes swung to the side of the grounds opposite the soldiers. Enthroned on a raised dais sat a man in the maroon garb of the soldiers, splendidly piped in gold, medals catching the glint of the setting sun. El Gaucho! Wentworth gazed at him curiously, but he was still too far away to see clearly. There was a plumed honor-guard of soldiers in shining cuirass and helmets about El Gaucho—a girl in flowing ceremonial robes on his left; on his right an arrogant man in a high, black shako like a Death's-Head Hussar…. But he would inspect those when he was closer to them. There were other things now to absorb his attention. Before the dais of El Gaucho, four huge draught horses were held motionless by eight grooms, one to each side of the bit. They had scarlet harness—a cross-tree lay at the heels of each.

A SENSE of uneasiness rippled over Wentworth and he frowned slightly. His eyes slanted to right and left, taking in two thick, stubby posts with a cross bar near the top which had been set deeply in the ground within thirty feet of the dais, on each side of the place where the horses stood. The posts were like crude crosses, like… the Spider's grim jaw set harshly. Suddenly he knew the reason for the brooding silence that hung over the field, the stiff waiting of the crowds. Those were flogging posts, and the horses… *Good God!* It couldn't be what he thought it was. Such barbarity as that had died in the sixteenth century!

He felt Barker's hand on his arm. "What's up, Spider?" he asked with worry in his tones. "I don't like the looks of things."

Wentworth shook his head. "I hope it's not what I think it is," he said flatly, "but whatever happens, keep that upper lip stiff."

"What do you mean?"

"Torture, Barker."

Wentworth heard the boy's breath suck in shudderingly. He said hoarsely, "The damned… fiends! Well, they won't get a squeak out of me."

"Of course not," said the Spider, making his voice light with an effort. "I'm probably all wrong, but it's as well to be prepared." He knew suddenly that he wasn't wrong and his throat closed dryly. Not for himself—torture had been tried on him before this, torture of the soul that is harder to bear than torture of the body. But this splendid boy! Tommy Barker was in this peril solely because he had risked his life to help the Spider. He must not suffer for that. He must not… Wentworth turned quietly to the guard on his right.

"Fall out and give my compliments to the officer. The prisoner wishes to speak to him," he said it quietly, but in the accent of command that comes only to those who have commanded. "Fall out!"

The soldier saluted mechanically, hesitated as he realized what he had done, then went at double-time, gun on shoulder, to the side of the officer. Wentworth saw the hesitation of the officer, then he dropped back and fell into step beside him.

"Be quick," he said. "What is it?"

"If it is to be torture," Wentworth said quietly, "I wish to appeal to El Gaucho for this boy with me. Let him inflict double penalties on me."

The officer looked down at the dusty ground beneath their feet as they marched along, stirring a slow gray mist from the earth; then he glanced at Wentworth.

"It is a man's request," he said somberly. "I'll do what I can."

Wentworth said, "Thank you."

Barker cried sharply, "No, no. I didn't understand. You can't do that, Spider."

The officer said harshly, "Quiet, prisoner." He rapidly overtook the leading platoon again and fell in position. The soldier who had dropped out to obey the Spider's order looked narrowly at him from the corner of his eyes. Strange that he had obeyed a prisoner, strange when it might have brought rebuke and sharp punishment upon his head. But he need not have felt disconcerted. Stronger men than he had obeyed the Spider and felt it honor to hear his commands.

Barker's hand came to Wentworth's arm again. "I won't permit that."

Wentworth said, "Quiet."

There was a brooding pain in his heart. He had small hope that El Gaucho would permit what he requested, but at least it might achieve the end of all this tearfulness that was intrinsic in this armed force El Gaucho had gathered about him. The Spider might succeed in snatching a gun and killing El Gaucho! Forlorn hope!

FOR WENTWORTH could see no escape for himself. It was likely that this man who called himself King and arrogated to himself regal powers, would have the flogging continued until Wentworth and Barker died. The Spider's mind harked back

101

to the cruelty of ancient days at sea when the cat-o'-nine-tails had been the instrument of harsh discipline. A short-shafted whip with nine lashes of rawhide stemming from it—the last two inches of each lash wound in brass wire and tipped with a leaden knout. A man had once survived a hundred lashes....

Yes, it would be better to make the effort to kill El Gaucho. In the anger afterward, soldiers might cut down both him and Barker....

In response to a sharp command, the soldiers about Wentworth and Barker took a stand to the left of the dais. The squad surrounding the ten gangsters who had flown west were flanking the dais on the opposite side. They stood like that, waiting, and the officer who commanded the squad braced himself and marched stalwartly to a position directly in front of the throne, dropped to one knee and bowed his bared head.

Wentworth watched the man and suddenly realized that he had asked a tremendous thing of this officer, that the man had gone with fear and trembling to carry his petition to El Gaucho. The Spider saw that the man spoke without lifting his head and he saw El Gaucho lean forward slightly, frowning. For the first time, then, he had a close sight of this man who was terrorizing the West, who now threatened to carry his pillaging, slaughtering host to destroy the East. His carriage was arrogant, the head shapely and proudly held. And the face was strong, intelligent, the profile like something on a coin. A full beard covered his mouth. The nose was aquiline, finely chiseled, and the eyes beneath smoothly arched brows were deep and wide—the eyes, Wentworth realized with a start, of a dreamer! Good God! A dreamer who slaughtered scores and could torture men with the ancient horror of the four horses!

El Gaucho lifted his hand and the officer rose, backed away for five paces before he arose, replaced his hat and right-faced to march to where Wentworth stood. He spoke sharply to the guard, and four soldiers removed their hats and handed them to comrades with their rifles, seized Wentworth's arms and marched him down the line of men. A feeling of sharp disappointment turned the Spider's heart to lead. There would be no weapon within his reach that he could grab, even if he could break the holds of these four men gripping his arms. He felt his hat snatched off, then the four men dropped to their knees, dragging him down also.

Wentworth did not bow his head and shoulders. He kneeled there as erectly as he could, facing El Gaucho. The eyes of the two met and held. What the Spider saw confirmed his distant judgment of the man. His eyes were those of a dreamer, but his gaze held command. There was something magnetic, too, about his personality. Neither man spoke for a long moment, then El Gaucho nodded shortly.

"If you hoped to have a chance to kill me by this audience," he said, "it's a hopeless attempt."

Irresistibly, the Spider smiled, but the expression was not amiable. His disguised face twisted into sinister, mocking lines.

"You reason soundly, Gaucho," he said pleasantly, "but my plea is sincere. The boy had no idea with what he was embroiling himself. He merely likes me personally as I admire him. He sought to do what he could to defend me, and had no intent of an assault upon your majesty."

A LOUD shout pulled the Gaucho's eyes to the left. It was Barker. "He lies! He lies!" Barker cried. "Don't listen to him, Gau...." A soldier's fist smashing against his lips stopped Barker's voice, and El Gaucho turned his face steadily back to Wentworth.

"The lad has courage," he said quietly, his voice firm, resonant. "You, too, have courage, Spider, but no man has ever needed to think twice about that." He hesitated, looking piercingly into Wentworth's face, then shook his head slowly. "That isn't your true face. It doesn't match your eyes. I could use men like you two in my company. There would be high places in my court, but the proffer would be useless, I know. You will be true to yourself though it means death."

A slow smile moved El Gaucho's bearded lips. "It is a pity you must die, Spider, without a sword in your hand."

The Spider's eyes held his. "I accept my fate," he said shortly. "I did not come before you to ask mercy for myself. But I did not think El Gaucho stooped to murder children."

El Gaucho jerked to his feet, red rage flashing from his eyes. "You dare!"

"Dare, hell," Wentworth returned laconically. "You're a cheap four-flusher, killing children like Barker to inflate your self-esteem!"

Two guards sprang forward with swords ripping from their sheaths, bright points glittering toward Wentworth's throat. Rage distorted their faces. It was the chance for which the

Spider had angled. With a violent wrench, he freed his right arm from the hands of the soldiers on that side. He crossed his right fist against the jaw of one of those on his left and slammed him against his companion.

Free then for the moment, he sprang to meet the two guards with their glittering swords drawn back to thrust. Behind them, he had a glimpse of El Gaucho, towering on the dais in his anger, of other guards jostling forward, while the insolent man in the black shako held an automatic ready in his right hand. The girl, whose face he had not seen until now, was leaning forward with her white hands clenched against her throat. It was impossible to tell whether it was fear or anxiety for... Wentworth suddenly realized that the woman wanted him to conquer! The sight of her intensely white face, her starry eyes, was a draught of courage to his lips.

Laughter leaped from his mouth and he sprang to meet the two guardsmen with their swords. They held them not in a fencing position but clenched at their sides for a stabbing thrust that would eliminate this mocker once and for all. As he sprang forward, Wentworth whipped his cape from his shoulders, hurled it in the face of the foremost guard. Instinctively, he flung up hands and sword to tear the blinding thing away and in that instant, Wentworth had his sword wrist. With a wrench he tore the weapon from the swordsman's grasp. His right arm had gone about the soldier's armored body and with the same movement, he hurled the fellow against his charging comrade.

A muffled scream tore from the man's cloak-covered face and his fellow guard's sword point protruded bloodily from his thigh.

It had taken no more than seconds, this struggle, then Went-worth was vaulting the ten feet to the dais with his sword ready in his right hand. He saw the gun of the man in the shako rise, saw the raised swords of guardsmen thrusting toward him and knew joyously that none of them could reach him in time to stop a death thrust. Nothing could stop him save… Even as Went-worth sprang to the first step of the dais with his saber licking out, El Gaucho's own sword whipped from its scabbard….

HERE WAS one thing, Wentworth knew, that could defeat him, and he realized in the first movement of El Gaucho's saber that this man, too, was a master swordsman. It was not that the Spider doubted his own ability to pierce that guard and kill, given a few moments, but he knew that before their blades had clashed a second time, death would be upon the Spider from behind. Useless to press his attack. A smile thinned his lips, death sat in his eyes.

"Dare you to fight me, man to man, El Gaucho?" he cried.

He drew back a pace, grounding the point of his saber and El Gaucho lowered his point, too, lifted his left hand to stop the assault upon Wentworth by the guards about him, by his right.

"Surrender the saber, Spider," he said calmly, "or you will be wounded, not killed, so that you will live for the whipping post. It would give me great pleasure, Spider, to meet you with swords, but it cannot be. My cause is greater than I. There must be…" He cut his words short with a lift of his left hand. "Surrender your sword, Spider."

What, had he lost then? Wentworth's proud, disdainful eyes swept the faces about him, saw their wrath, met the pity and the admiration in the eyes of the woman, and saw there was no chance. El Gaucho, with that blade in his hand, was invulnerable since there were so many others to strike Wentworth down from behind. The Spider shrugged, disguising his despair with a smile. He lifted the blade above his head with both hands and brought its flat side down across his knee, snapping the steel off sheer.

"It was a good try, Spider," said El Gaucho, smiling.

Wentworth laughed bitterly, felt soldiers' hands seize his arms violently again and drag him backward. He had failed, and with his effort he had doomed Barker, too. His laughter died on his lips. The sacrifice was necessary. If it meant Barker's death now, there at least had been a chance that he might save hundreds—thousands—of others from sharing the fate of so many who had perished in El Gaucho's bloody raids.

He held his head proudly, defiantly as he was marched back to Barker. Ropes were wound about his arms now, locking them behind him, and the officer stared angrily at him. He said nothing, but there was hatred in his eyes, hatred and a touch, too, of fear. The glance made the Spider's lips curve in self-mockery. No man need fear him now. Death was near, ignoble death, and yonder sat a man who would be too strong, too mighty for all the forces of law and order. Triumph sat upon his head like an accolade.

Wentworth lifted his eyes to the sunset fires of the skies. There must—*there must*—be some power greater than this El Gaucho....

CHAPTER 9
GAUCHO JUSTICE

THE UPROAR occasioned by the Spider's attack upon El Gaucho faded swiftly. Once more the brooding silence of those who wait for death settled over the parade grounds. The sun was a baleful red eye upon the horizon which seemed strangely appropriate to the horror that was to come. Wentworth stood erect, with set face and grimly gazing eyes, beside Barker, who, he had seen, was bound also.

"You shouldn't have done that, Spider—tried to save me," Barker whispered softly. "You might have known it was no dice."

Wentworth nodded slightly. "It was the only chance. I had to," he said shortly. "Is that the girl?"

Barker's voice sank to a whisper. "Isn't she glorious?"

The Spider nodded again. She was lovely enough with her truly regal bearing and her starry eyes beneath the black crown of her hair. But that was not what he was thinking. If he could survive or escape the torture that impended, would she be willing to help? If not for the sake of aiding doomed men, then for the sake of this fine boy at his side? The woman beside El Gaucho was no older than Tommy Barker, for all her stern, straight-backed poise. Possibly she was a year or two younger....

Wentworth's course of thought broke as he caught the muffled tap of drums. He lifted his eyes to behold a new squad of soldiers approaching from a small, white house which had barred windows. Amid them, one marched who was not in uniform, whose bare shoulders rose above those of the others.

He was uttering a thin, despairing, wailing sound. It was scarcely human, the whine that rose from that poor wretch. It was the cry a suffering animal might make....

Barker said, "Good God, what is that?"

Wentworth did not answer. Why tell Barker that this was the sound that is made by tortured men, suffering pain beyond the ability of man to endure?

Barker's breath was noisy in his mouth. "They're taking him to the horses! What are they going to do to him with horses?"

Three men walked in front of the squad, a man in a black robe with a scarlet cap that covered his entire head and face. Behind him walked two men stripped to the waist, their arms folded across thick-muscled chests. Each bore in his right hand the short haft of a cat-o'-nine-tails, its leaded lashes slapping gently against their thighs. And as they came nearer, the four horses were being maneuvered by the eight grooms, backed together so that each great gray Percheron formed with its body the corner of a square. They were led slightly apart, the cross-trees dragging at their heels.

The marching squad was very near now and the man they led began to strain and lurch against the grasp of his captors. He was weak—too weak to escape. Already, Wentworth surmised, he had felt the cunning work of the torturers. For him, this would only be a final, insupportable agony before the blessed release of death. The soldiers halted beside the horses and the two torturers thrust whips into their belts, seized the luckless victim. The soldiers were white-faced, a little uncertain in their step as they marched away. Wentworth glanced cautiously at the men to either side and they were sick-faced, too. A chance to escape? The Spider shook his head. Not with bound arms, not with all these hundreds surrounding him.

Barker was moaning. "Oh lord! Look at that man's chest! Why—why… they've *burned* him! It's burned black!"

"Quiet, Barker," Wentworth snapped. "Quiet!"

THE BOY moved closer for a moment, but soldiers yanked him away again. "Stand still, you!" Their fear and their nausea was reflected in the savagery of their voices. Their quaking made them cruel. The torturers held the man there beside the horses and a soldier stepped forward, sword swaying against his side, began to read in a drone that nevertheless carried emphatically over the hushed parade grounds.

"… A traitor to the cause," rang his voice. "He deserted his post in Jackson City…."

Wentworth's lips curved in a hard thin smile. The Spider was leaning forward as if to go to the man's rescue, but what purpose could it serve? He knew it was useless, but he gazed at the wretched victim of El Gaucho and his eyes were cold. He would watch—and someday, somehow, he would wreak his vengeance upon this Gaucho! A while ago, Wentworth had felt a nascent admiration for the man's conduct and courage. This torture, too, had a purpose, of course. It was discipline, designed to hold the men in line against all danger and temptation with the certainty that, if they wavered, this same death awaited them. He knew its reason, but he was sure that there must be a deep-seated cruelty in the soul of a man who would permit such things.

The wretch tried to drop on his knees, to beg for mercy, but the torturers held him erect. Abruptly they slammed him to the ground and bound thongs about his wrists and ankles. While he screamed horribly, they fastened one limb in turn to the harness of each of the four horses. The grooms who held the horses faced away from where the man lay, stroking the Percherons, calming them with caresses. The torturers stepped away and the scarlet-masked executioner moved forward....

Barker sobbed, the sounds strangled in his throat. He gasped out words. "Oh, God! Oh God! They're going... going to *pull him to pieces!*"

WENTWORTH'S BOUND fists were aching knots behind him as the shrill toneless shrieking of that man, helpless on the ground among the four horses, pierced his ears. Barker had named it. When the weight of those mighty horses was put upon the harness, the man's limbs would be slowly, slowly torn from his body while he still lived. In spite of himself, the Spider took a slow step forward, but soldiers' hands jerked him backward. Barker was shouting meaningless sounds, too, until a soldier mercifully slapped his head with the butt of his gun. It was not hard enough to knock the boy out, but it stunned him so that he swayed, dazed, on his feet in the grip of the soldiers. He was silenced.

The executioner lifted his hand, and the four men who held the horses attached to the victim's arms made the Percherons lean gently into their harness. The straps straightened, tautened. If the screams before had been heart-rending, those that rose now were enough to tear the soul of God. Wentworth, steeling himself, his jaw set, the tendons of his neck rigid, saw blood spurt from the man's wrists and shoulders, from his ankles. The executioner lifted his hand again and the horses eased in their harness. It was not, then, that he was merely to be pulled to pieces. That was not sufficient torture. He was to be allowed, too, the agony of dislocated arms and legs.

Wentworth's soul squeezed out a curse between his set teeth. He pulled his eyes away from the scene. To either side of him, men stood rigidly, some with their eyes closed, some shaken with fear and agony. A soldier reeled out of line and fell, his body wracked with nausea. Wentworth's gaze sought out El Gaucho. Impassively, unmoving, leaning slightly forward in an attitude of interest, El Gaucho sat upon his throne watching the torture which was enacted before him.

A new, shrill cry came from the tortured man. It was weaker, hoarser, without meaning except for its inarticulate agony. The girl on the left side of the throne was leaning against the chair, her hand covering her eyes. But she could not stop her ears. El Gaucho turned toward her and his lips moved. The girl stood rigidly, her hand dropping from before her eyes and… the man screamed again.

So piercing, so wracking, was the cry that Wentworth's eyes were pulled involuntarily toward the torture. The gray horses were startled, half-frightened by the cries that seemed to issue from the earth at their very heels. They tried to turn their great heads to look at this gibbering thing behind them, but the grooms gentled them, patted their necks with hands that trembled in spite of themselves. At a gesture from the executioner, they once more eased the strain for a moment while the screams died to a babbling moan. Then they began again a slow, forward pull, all four horses straining together, horses that weighed a ton apiece, straining their powerful muscles.

The rays of the setting sun seemed to gild them with the blood of their victim, great gentle beasts goaded into a fearful killing by kind, patting hands. But the red of the sun could not match the hot crimson that was spurting now from the lump of flesh that had been human....

Barker had recovered full consciousness now and, shuddering from head to foot, clung to one of the soldiers for support, though that man, too, was trembling. Many of the spectators were like that and the Spider knew that nothing save fear of a similar fate held them subject to El Gaucho. Even among the guards and officers who surrounded the throne, faces were deathly pale....

At last there was such a cry that even the Spider's iron control slipped for a moment and his body bounded against the ropes, against the restraining hands of soldiers. But it was already too late, irreparably too late. The straining horses trembled and reared against the drag of that screaming thing behind them. No groom's hand could gentle them now. One of them broke free of the men who held him, galloped headlong away across the parade ground, dragging a crimson something in the swirling dust behind him. No one tried to stop the horse. One of the men who had been in charge of him dropped where he stood, a limp, unconscious figure. Little rills and streams of blood from that other still thing puddled the dust about him.

There was still a twitching, still some ghost of sound issuing from that mangled flesh, but the horses, standing, trembling now beneath the caresses of their grooms, had done their work. The man was dismembered....

THERE WAS a great aching silence following the last shrieks of a man horribly dying. El Gaucho stepped down slowly, deliberately, from his throne, walked close to where at last that twitching human thing was silent. His deep voice matched his great frame. It boomed forth gigantically:

"You have seen a traitor die, my people," he roared. *"Remember!"*

Just that, followed by awed silence. Then one of the officers lifted a hand, and from the stricken hundreds there came a broken, hoarse salute:

"Hail! El Gaucho! Hail!"

CHAPTER 10
PROMISE OF DEATH

AFTER THE last shout had died, people began to slip away. There was none of the confused sounds, none of the talking which usually attends the break-up of a crowd. Each one stole away as if he sought to avoid observation—as if some fearful, vengeful god watched gloatingly.

The little group of officers remained with El Gaucho, and the soldiers stood fast while the torturers tossed what was left of their victim into a bag for a servant to drag away. In the silence that followed, El Gaucho's voice, addressing the girl beside him, was clearly audible to Wentworth.

"I did not think you would have so weak a heart, Carollotta," he said, "when justice was being done."

The girl laid a flowerlike hand on the arm of the throne and swayed a little on her feet. "Justice!" she whispered. The sound hissed out into the gathering dusk.

"A useful lesson in justice, my niece," El Gaucho's voice was deep, grave. "You must remember that you have a high destiny. You will be the mother of the Line, the new royalty founded by my blood. It is for this reason I require you to meet more than ordinary women can stand. Your beauty is a glorious thing to pass on to the blood; but a soldier's heart must go with it!"

Wentworth felt the anger of the boy beside him. He glared at El Gaucho, and the wish rose overwhelmingly in his heart that he had succeeded in that reckless dash with the sword. Even if he had afterward died by the torture of the horses, it would have been worth it to strike down the author of so much infamy. The muffled tap of drums came again and, despite himself, Wentworth's head pulled toward the sound to see what new torture portended. The executioner with his scarlet cowl marched as before ahead of the two men with the many-shaped whips. Wentworth's shoulder muscles corded. This time they came—*for him!*

Carollotta's voice rang out behind him in a frightened cry. "Oh, uncle," she implored. "No more today! In heaven's name, no more today!"

Wentworth's eyes were fixed in a fascination he could not break on the two broad-shouldered torturers with their lead-tipped whips.

"No, no, uncle!" cried the girl. "These men have done nothing to you. They are the enemies of the gangsters. Why should you exact vengeance? They have done nothing, nothing…!"

"Nothing," drawled El Gaucho amusedly, "except make an attempt on our lives!"

Wentworth felt the quivering of Barker, close against his shoulder now. "Why does she do that?" he whispered. "She won't accomplish anything. Only make it tough for herself…."

Wentworth forced his eyes away from the torturers to gaze on the girl. She had drawn herself up scornfully, her head with its plaited coronet of smooth black hair defiantly lifted.

"You call yourself king!" she said contemptuously. "Yet you quibble with the truth! Why not admit that you like to see men tortured?"

"Silence, woman!" thundered El Gaucho. "The man is an assassin!"

Carollotta laughed musically. "Yes, my uncle," she agreed, "but you had determined on his torture *before you ever saw him*. Why then equivocate? Why pretend that the torture is because of what happened here? Is this the vaunted justice of King Carlos of Bethania?"

SHE WAS silent, gazing scornfully at the man before the throne. There was not even the movement of a foot among the guard of officers about the throne. There were white, fearful faces there, startled eyes gazing straight ahead. Across the parade grounds the squad of soldiers marched on with muffled drums, and the dull thudding of the drums was like the beating of a great cosmic heart, slow, heavy, portentous.

El Gaucho's eyes remained locked with those of the girl who had defied him, and it was he who first turned swaying, bowing his head as if in thought. One foot was placed forward a little; his right hand was thrust in the breast of his coat. He made a brooding somber picture. Wentworth tried to appraise him coldly, but hatred prodded his brain with sharp hot points.

This Gaucho, this Carlos, who called himself King of Bethania, believed himself far above the average man; a super-being, almost godlike, Wentworth decided. And because he had the will and the strength, because he was gifted with the personality that commands, he was dangerously near what he believed. No ordinary man could have assembled this force of men and held them strongly in leash to do his bidding.

Abruptly, El Gaucho's head came up. He spun toward the man who had stood throughout the scene at his right hand, the man with the black shako of the Death's-Head Hussars.

"Von Hapszollern," he asked dryly, "will you have those two men brought before me again?"

Wentworth gazed at the man called Von Hapszollern and a start of surprise jerked at his muscles. He knew that protruding lower lip; that prominent nose and black eyes. By the gods! It was Prince Wilhelm of Ruthia! Wentworth had been presented at a reception in the Prince's honor in New York four years ago. The Spider prodded his memory, recalling the man's country, Ruthia, a tiny key state in the Balkans—and he remembered, too, the whereabouts of Bethania. Bethania was a republic neighboring on the other state… Wentworth's eyes flashed back to Prince Wilhelm.

Machine guns were
stuttering as the untrained
men dropped....

"Pardon, your majesty," said Wilhelm, swaggering forward a little, "do you think this is wise? These two men are extremely dangerous. You have seen already how this—er... a—vermin behaves. The whip would be good for them and"—he leaned closer, whispering. Wentworth read his lips easily—"It would be a salutary lesson for these others of whom we know little."

Carollotta's face turned even paler. "My uncle, consider your justice!"

"Why should two soldiers," growled Wilhelm, "listen to a girl? Come, let us decide this as it should be."

Wentworth turned his head slightly toward Barker, and a smile touched his lips. "That does it," he whispered. "We will be spared."

Barker frowned in bewilderment, but El Gaucho's deep booming voice, thick with anger, confirmed the Spider's keen estimate of his character.

" 'Let us,' did you say, Wilhelm?" El Gaucho thundered. "Prince, you forget yourself!"

Wilhelm drew himself up, but it was obvious that El Gaucho's manner intimidated him. He stammered and retreated before the glare of the man. El Gaucho turned deliberately to Carollotta, bowed over her white hand.

"My niece, I thank you," he said gravely. "My justice is more imperative than the need to chastise dogs."

He turned back to Wilhelm, speaking more pleasantly. "I give my niece into the hands of her affianced," he said. "Will you see her to the ladies' quarters?"

PRINCE WILHELM took his dismissal with ill grace, but

he could not object. Wentworth stared in amazement, heard the sharp low cursing of Barker at the information that it was to this stripling of Ruthia's royalty that the girl, Carollotta, had been pledged in marriage. Abruptly, Wentworth saw the whole setup. It was fairly clear now that El Gaucho sought in his American crimes the money to restore himself to his Bethanian throne. The girl was to be used to bind him in peace to his neighboring state. Good God, what a colossal egoist the man was! So that he might place himself on his throne again, he organized criminals to ravage an entire countryside, killed hundreds of fellow men ruthlessly! And the heady wine of power had gone to his head. He dreamed now of world dominion!

If only Washington knew what portended. A few companies of United States Marines could wipe out this camp of bandits in quick time. But no one yet realized the immensity of El Gaucho's activities. Troops had not even been called out by the governors. And if they were, what would it accomplish? Many of the National Guard would be green to actual warfare and though officered by men of war experience, they would still be civilians, unused to discipline. And El Gaucho's army had been recruited from border badmen....

El Gaucho mounted his throne deliberately and sent for the gangsters under Peterson's leadership. Peterson swaggered up to the throne, tossed a hand in jaunty salute.

"How're yuh, Gauch?" He started to step up on the dais to shake hands. A short, stocky man in the armor of the guards stepped forward violently, hurled him backward so that Peterson almost fell. The gangster snarled, his hand flashed to his coat lapel. Then, remembering he was without arms, he turned white.

The stocky man in cuirass and helmet stood furiously before him, broad German face twisted in anger.

"Do not shpeak, *Schwein,*" he growled, "until you are shpoken to!"

Peterson was not without courage, whatever his faults. He stepped up close to the officer and tapped the cuirass with a stiff forefinger.

"Listen, punk," he said flatly, his veneer of suave speech gone. "Don't try any funny business with me or you'll run into the dirty end of a chopper...."

Peterson's voice cut short, for another guardsmen stepped up behind him and clapped a large, competent hand over his mouth. Four more guardsmen confronted the other disarmed gangsters with naked swords, and the criminals wilted.

The officer's thick voice instructed Peterson unemotionally. "Do not shpeak unless you are first addressed, *Schwein.*"

He lifted a hand and the guard who had seized Peterson from behind stepped back a pace, drew his sword and presented its point to the gangster's back.

"If he shpeaks out of turn again... remind him," said the officer, and stepped back to his former position beside the throne.

"That is well, De Moltkez," said El Gaucho, eyeing Peterson.

The officer, De Moltkez, saluted with a wide sweep of his hand and automaton precision. Wentworth's lips lifted at the corners in spite of himself at Peterson's rebuke, but the smile quickly faded as Peterson presented the proposal of the gang-sters.

He used a remarkably humble voice, battling against the anger that shook him. He told of the fortunes to be had in the East, of the ease with which police could be evaded. Then he itemized the loosely coupled groups of criminals whom, in making this plea, he represented. They were all "big shots," he declared. They had the political powers "sewed up."

"Why, when some of the Spider's pals," he went on, "busted into one of our minor headquarters in New York to rescue him, we just had to tell the police to skip out and they did."

HE PAUSED a moment, apparently trying to estimate what impression he had made upon El Gaucho. Obviously, discon-certed by his treatment, he tried to build himself large with words. When he paused, El Gaucho's face was as inscrutable as ever.

"What we need, your majesty," Peterson rushed on, "is a man like you, who can lead. A king. The big shots out East saw what you did here and it was great stuff. No kidding. You make us all look like pikers. Now, if you'll come East and run the works, there won't be anybody can stop us. We'll own the country! And don't think you can do it without us. We know the ropes, and we know… other things."

El Gaucho said gently, "What other things, for instance?"

Peterson sucked in a deep breath. "We big shots don't like competition," he said slowly. "Maybe you've heard of being taken for a ride?"

There was a breathless silence then, while guards and officers watched El Gaucho. Wentworth's own eyes narrowed with attention. Peterson had shown more courage than he had expected. How would El Gaucho take this quite definite threat? It would show to a large extent just how great he was, or how great he thought himself. And Wentworth saw. El Gaucho merely moved his bearded lips in a smile.

"We are too occupied just now," he said gravely, "to give your proposition due deliberation. In the morning we are taking Grand Junction, a town just south of here. Tomorrow night, we will give you our decision."

El Gaucho's answer was entirely adequate. He merely smiled at the threat, made a courteous, but utterly confident reply. It was as if the matter were too trivial for notice. Wentworth caught that, realized anew the man's power. But his thoughts were swept away to the slaughter and pillage that impended and which El Gaucho had mentioned so casually. *In the morning we are taking Grand Junction...* And Wentworth saw something else. He saw that the officer of the guards, who was called De Moltkez, had stepped back from the throne and was in close conversation with Prince Wilhelm. The two men's eyes were on Wentworth and it needed no lip-reading to tell what they planned.

"...kill them quietly," Wilhelm was saying. "After the battle, Carlos will have forgotten...."

A sharp determination shot through Wentworth, battling with the hopelessness of his and Barker's position. He must escape and race to the rescue of Grand Junction. With a warning, the citizens could barricade their streets and fight off the regiment of bandits. But to accomplish that, he would have to evade not only the soldiers, but also the assassins whom De Moltkez and Wilhelm would send to destroy them.... Even while Wentworth considered plans, he was thrust forward by a soldier. He realized that El Gaucho had ordered them away. He and Barker were thrown alone into the tiny, whitewashed jail with its barred windows.

The jail's walls were of thick, squared logs and the chinks were filled with cement. The windows.... They were impossible. Wentworth's jaw set stubbornly. He would, he *must* escape. He spun toward Barker. The boy was seated on one of the two iron cots that were the room's sole furniture. His face was alight, his smile wide. His mind was elsewhere. Wentworth wavered. Should he tell him about what threatened, the grim future that lay before them? Slowly, he shook his head.

"You saw her, Spider," Barker said. "Did you ever see anyone to compare with her, did you? Gee, she's wonderful! And she smiled at me. She smiled at me! You noticed that?"

"I noticed," said Wentworth dryly, "that she is to be married to Prince Wilhelm of Ruthia. What chance do you suppose you have? A fine chance to get pulled to pieces by horses, that's all. You heard El Gaucho? He'll marry her to the sour Teutonic sausage who's the simon-pure crown prince of Ruthia.... Better think of some of the girls you went to school with."

BARKER WAVED a hand airily. "Nuts to that. I tell you she smiled at me." He stretched out on the cot, and put his hands behind his head, grinning at the ceiling. Wentworth smiled at him gently. His heart was heavy with foreboding. He felt sure that El Gaucho would throw in with Peterson, even if it were only to gain control of the gangs the gangster nominally headed. What happened to Peterson after that union did not matter. The gangs were only loosely affiliated now, could easily be smashed by the right attack, but once they were bound together under the iron hand of El Gaucho…!

Orderlies brought two tin buckets of simple fare with bread and water in crocks to complete it. The last rays of the sun had faded from the bare wall opposite their one barred window, when they finished eating and presently Wentworth heard the soft, regular breathing of his companion. When, Wentworth wondered, would the assassins come? He climbed up to test the bars of the windows. They were firm and had been recently erected. Probably they were tool steel. Impossible to attack them with any but the best of instruments, and the Spider had been stripped of all the devices with which usually he could force his way out. It must rest with strategy then.

He crossed to the barred grating of the cell, looked through the narrow antechamber to the outside door of this log hut. A sentry paced back and forth at regular, short intervals. There was another guard beneath the cell window. Wentworth timed the passing of the sentries and worked silently, swiftly, when they were not in sight. He filled the tin pails in which their dinner had come with water and drinking jugs. Then he balanced them to hang on spoons which were thrust into the frame just above the cell door. He ripped strips from his shirt to make a cord which he attached to them. He laid his blanket on the floor just inside the door and tied a stronger cord, made of a strip of the blanket itself, to that. Then he lay down to wait. Feeble artifices, but they would have to serve. He was quite sure that the assassins would not risk the noise of shooting, and it would be next to impossible to throw a knife between the bars of either door or window. That means that Prince Wilhelm's killers would have to enter the cell through the door. When they did....

Wentworth lay down upon his cot, holding the ends of the two improvised cords and pretended to sleep. He had not apprised Barker of his plans, for it was doubtful if the boy would be able to fake sleep, to remain quiet and wait for the killers....

The long watches of the night dragged on. The sergeant of the guard made his rounds, and the challenges rang out clearly on the thin, chill air of the plains. It was a half hour after the sergeant passed that the sentry in front of the cell house challenged sharply. There was a muttered colloquy, then three men slipped in through the outer door. Despite his preparedness, Wentworth felt his body stiffening and he had to force himself to resume the deep regular breathing of sleep. His hand was alert on the cords attached to his feeble traps. In the dimness of the outer room, he caught the gleam of steel. Two of the men carried swords in their hands. The third hung back as they advanced. Wentworth's face became set and grim. They knew their work, these three. That one who hung back would carry a revolver and in extremity, he would use it on "escaping" prisoners.

As silently as shadows, the two assassins drifted to the door and peered for long seconds between the bars. Wentworth blessed the deep, noisy sleep of Barker for its naturalness. It covered up any discrepancies in his own imitation. There was a tautness in his nerves. Everything depended on his own swift action at the right moment. Barker could be counted on to spring to the attack when he was aroused....

THE LOCK rasped faintly in its socket, the door pivoted on oiled hinges. For a breath, the two men hung back, as if some fear stayed them from immediate entrance; then they came in together. The man in front took a long stride into the room, then checked, staring down at the softness of the blanket which he felt beneath his feet. It was the moment for which Wentworth had waited. He snapped erect and, putting his whole weight into a single heave, yanked at the cords fastened to blanket and to the dinner pails, loaded with water, the scraps of the dinner and the water crocks!

The tin pails struck upon the head and shoulders of the second man. The one in front was thrown to his back by the sudden yank upon the blanket on which he stood. His sword hand flew high, a choked cry in his throat.

"Barker!" Wentworth cried. "We're attacked!"

While he shouted, he was leaping forward. It was no trick to take the sword from the man who sprawled upon the floor, but the second assassin was already recovering from the blow of pails upon his head and shoulders. His sword licked out to meet the saber Wentworth had captured. Twice the steel rang, then the Spider lunged savagely and sliced through the other's guard.

Even as his thrust went home, he felt the arms of the man he had upset close about his legs. The Spider dropped to his knees and the sword, wedged between his victim's ribs, broke off short in his hand.

"Don't let him lock the door, Barker!" Wentworth cried. "Hold the door."

He had a glimpse of Barker springing for the steel door, then he was locked in a life-and-death struggle with the man who had tripped him. The man had a dagger. Wentworth had two inches of blade on the hilt of the saber, blunt ended, nearly useless. He dodged a stab and his left hand darted to the man's throat. With a cry of pain, the assassin reeled to his feet. For a moment then, the two stood face to face in the darkness. Wentworth could see the gleam of the man's teeth and his own lips curved in a savage smile. Barker was tussling there in the antechamber with the third assassin and the alarm of the sentries— two rifle shots crashing into the sky—sounded like thunder. It would have to be fast now, or all would be lost. And that, to the Spider, meant not only his own life but also the scores who would die in Grand Junction tomorrow if he did not escape; the hundreds who would die throughout the United States if he failed to smash this conspiracy.

With a shout, he sprang toward his enemy, saw the knife slice upward for his belly, a blow almost impossible to parry. He could take a chance at striking it aside with his left fist.... Instead, Wentworth sprang to the right, hitting for the face with the abbreviated stub of his saber. The man flinched back and they were squared off again. Despite the masking darkness, the movements of steel caught glints of light and betrayed the whereabouts of each. The Spider pressed in. There could be no delay. Delay would mean victory for his assailant. And the man seemed to realize that. Feinted about in the darkness. He snatched up a blanket from Barker's cot and flapped it toward Wentworth to blind him.

The Spider laughed. He caught the blanket in the air and yanked violently, springing forward and to the left of the assassin. The man realized his mistake too late. He cried out despairingly, stumbled, threw his arms wide… and the Spider struck with the saber hilt. The broken blade, with all his weight and strength behind it, slipped behind the man's upthrown arm and caught him just back of the jaw in the soft, fatal spot beneath the ear.

WENTWORTH DID not wait to see the results of that blow. He did not need to, for the man's life blood was spurting out from his jugular. Through the open door of the cell, the Spider sprang, pausing a moment to snatch up the sword of the first man he had killed. Barker reeled to his feet from the body of the officer.

"Good work, Barker," Wentworth said crisply. He stood and ran his hand over the floor, searching vainly for the man's revolver. No time to hunt, though the weapon would have increased their chances a hundred-fold. Sword ready in his hand, Wentworth leaped to the outer door. A rifle blazed at him at almost contact range, but his hand had jolted up its barrel just in time. The sword slid in under it and they were out of the jail house. The sentry died in his tracks.

Over by the tents, a bugle was blaring: "To arms!" Wentworth tossed the sword to Barker, snatched up the sentry's bayoneted rifle. He led a sprint toward the parade grounds and the house of El Gaucho. That was still his first goal, the death of that evil genius. As he and Barker sallied from the shadow of the jail, a running squad of men, rifles at port, smashed into them.

Wentworth pivoted and the rifle blasted from his hip, blew a soldier back upon his comrades. The bayonet licked out, and another fell. Barker's sword in his inexperienced hand, smashed down on another man's shoulder. Then a bayonet parried the saber, brushed it aside.

"Take them alive!" an officer shouted from somewhere behind. "Take them alive!"

It was just in time to stop a bayonet thrust which had Barker cold. The tip raked up the side of the boy's face, but he only growled in his throat and went in with the sword before him like a lance. The soldier who had spared him died. Wentworth fired once more and with his next shot, the hammer clicked on the empty chamber. He had snatched the rifle from the guard who had fired the alarm!

He was viciously engaged with two men who wielded the bayonet like experts. If they had heard the order to take the prisoners alive, it apparently meant nothing whatsoever to them. They were thrusting savagely for throat and belly. The Spider sprang to his right, so that one antagonist blocked the other. His first lunge stretched one soldier on the earth. The second man retreated and was finished with a point in his throat. Wentworth saw that Barker was down on his face, and a burning rage seethed up within him. He sprang to the rescue. Three men with bayonets pivoted to meet him. The officer stood to one side with sword in hand—and around a corner of the jail came a platoon of men at double quick march!

For a moment, Wentworth hesitated. All his heart dictated that he fight over the fallen body of this brave lad, though he knew it to be futile. Probably Barker was still alive. His sword would not have been too formidable against men with bayonets. The butt end of a rifle would have put him out. And rifle butts do not always kill... His desire was to stand by the unconscious lad on the ground....

But the Spider could not tarry.

Bitterness like the taste of ashes was in his soul. A town and a nation would lie at the mercy of murderers if he were slain or captured tonight, if he remained to help this brave boy....With a curse, Wentworth spun and ran into the dark gloom that lay upon the parade grounds.

"Halt!" cried the officer. "Halt, or we fire!"

WENTWORTH RAN on, zigzagging. There were only three riflemen in a position to fire. They were panting from their exertions and it was doubtful if they could hold a bead on a moving figure in the darkness. The platoon coming at the double would have to swing out of the column, the front rank drop to their knees, before they could fire. It would take a couple of seconds and those seconds counted with Wentworth. He detached the bayonet from the gun as he raced and dropped the useless rifle behind him. He quickened his stride directly toward the mansion of El Gaucho!

No lights there, no lights anywhere to guide the bullets. Fifty yards away from the riflemen, whose lead was beginning to sing through the night, Wentworth turned at right angles to his course and plunged for the tents of the soldiers bivouacked to southward. The dark cloak of the night was his salvation. He heard the rifle fire cease, heard the beat of soldiers' feet moving double quick across the parade grounds toward El Gaucho's home.

It had been deliberate, the rush toward the mansion. Soldiers would search the place, and fail to find him. When he finally went there, as he intended presently to do, he would not be expected. He ceased his running, crept up to the tents and lay at full length in the shadows between two of them. His breathing quieted slowly, but his mind raced on. It would be useless to attempt tonight to free Barker. There would be an overwhelming guard and in seeking to help his friend, he probably would find only death for himself. And the Spider's life was incalculably precious now. He knew damaging things about El Gaucho. If he could only kill the man, get clear of the camp....

Wentworth dug the point of his bayonet deep into the earth until it was clean and bright, fondled it in his hands. A slim weapon against a regiment of killers! The whole thing suddenly seemed fantastic to him. On the plains of the middle west, what state he did not know, he lay in the midst of a camp that the government did not guess existed, with a commander they thought merely a common bandit. The G-men would be after him, without a doubt, and they were efficient, but they were often slow in action. And they would have no force competent to cope with this terror. It was work for an army—or for a single man!

Wentworth got cautiously to his feet. The search of the

Gaucho's house had ended. There would be double sentries now—ceaseless patrolling.

The Spider's eyes were narrow and hard as he stole toward the house of El Gaucho with the bayonet covered in his cloak lest its gleam betray him. One thing they would not expect, that any fugitive would further endanger himself by a deliberate attack upon the generalissimo of their forces! Well, it would be death for one of them when they met, and the Spider had trained himself to kill....

CHAPTER 11
WHEN FOES MEET

THE MANSION, when the Spider peered at it from the middle of its fragrant flower garden, was only lightly guarded and unlighted. Two sentries made a slow circuit. That, apparently, was all. Wentworth waited until the two men had met and started back on their rounds away from him. Then he raced swiftly forward, hid close to the building.

When the two guards returned, they stood a moment talking idly.

"Damned shame we couldn't be in on this raid," one of them said.

"Yeah," the other grunted. "Gaucho must be a quarter of the way there by now. He'll wait, to have his men in place before it gets light."

"Sure, but that's what I hate, that waiting for the banks to open."

The two shouldered their rifles, and went back to their rounds again. Wentworth crouched, unmoving. With El Gaucho gone, there was no hope of a quick, all-conquering blow. There remained then only to dash for Grand Junction, to warn the town.... The opening of a window above where he crouched against the foundations of the building startled him. He shrank close against the wall, peered upward, saw a woman's hands clasped upon the sill. He held his breath, waiting, and the sentries paced back slowly.

"Sentry!" the woman called. It was Carollotta!

The sentry brought his gun to present arms. "Yes, Princess?"

"Sentry, the escaped prisoner is directly under my window!"

Her cry was stultifying, but Wentworth caught its import the moment the word "escaped" passed her lips. He was in action before the stiffly standing sentry could grasp her meaning. The sentry glimpsed a black cloaked figure springing from the shadows. He tried to bring his bayonet into position, but it was already too late. Wentworth's own bayonet whistled through the air and its dull edge caught the sentry behind the ear, hurled him unconscious to the ground. The other soldier was running forward with his bayonet leveled and the Spider awaited his coming. Then, sharply, his arm jerked upward from his side and the bayonet, butt-first, caught the man between the eyes and spilled him, also, senseless to the earth.

Wentworth snatched up a rifle and, in a long stride, was beneath the window with the needle point of the bayonet lifted to touch the white throat of the princess!

"Don't make a sound, Carollotta," he said quietly.

The woman looked down on him contemptuously. "You are a coward and a traitor," she said scornfully. "You deserted Tom Barker."

The words hurt Wentworth.

"I feel the same way about it," he said heavily, "but it was a matter of leaving him or getting warning to Grand Junction before your uncle strikes there. It was one life against many."

Carollotta said, "You deserted your friend!"

The Spider's voice was bitter. "Yes, I deserted my friend! I have deserted many friends so that I might fulfill my duty. I have deserted the woman I love, too, on occasion to fates more horrible than mere death by torture. I have done all those things."

"You sound… bitter," said Carollotta.

The Spider laughed shortly. "Tell me, Carollotta, where I may find guns and a horse."

Carollotta took the bayonet between her fingers and moved it aside. Wentworth let it waver and she leaned down toward him with her forearms on the sill.

"Stay," she whispered. "Stay and I will hide you. We will find means to free Tom Barker and…."

"… And," Wentworth interrupted flatly, "let a dozen—a score of people be killed in Grand Junction!"

CAROLLOTTA'S BREATH caught between her bitten lips. She started to speak, then stood stiffly at the window. Her hair was about her shoulders in two long, soft braids and fell across the silken weight of her negligee. She was very lovely, very young with the soft dusk of night about her. How could she realize the bitter philosophy of the Spider?

Carollotta said, "Oh it is hard, hard! I know you are right...."
She bent forward. "Hurry before I change my mind. There are
guns here in the house. My horse is stabled behind—a bay
mare called... Wilhemina. See, Spider, I trust you. You are my
only hope. In God's name—in the name of whatever you hold
sacred—come back and save... *my love!*"

Wentworth tossed the rifle to the ground, sprang to the sill
and drew himself inside. He stood gazing at Carollotta, then he
lifted her white hand to his lips.

"I will come back," he said simply. *"The Spider swears it!"*

He felt her small, soft fingers cling to his hand....

Wentworth strapped on two shoulder holsters with forty-
five automatics in them, dropped spare clips into his pockets.
He put two thirty-eight revolvers in the waist band of his trousers, girded on a keen-edged saber whose balance delighted his
heart. He had to kill a sentry to take Carollotta's mare. Then
he disappeared into the night, soft-footing toward the South
where lay Grand Junction and where the marauding army of El
Gaucho soon would spring its trap. He rode to his duty, but his
heart was heavy within him. The Spider must succeed tonight
and the Spider must not die. Too many hopes, too many hearts
hung upon the success of his ventures.

But Wentworth was not one to contemplate failure. Once out
of hearing of the camp, he gave the mare her head. There was
so little time to reach Grand Junction, fifteen miles away, and
prepare the town to resist an armed invasion. So little time—for
already there was in the East the hint of gray which is the false
dawn. The Spider leaned far forward on the horse's withers to

ease his weight, guiding her in the darkness with a firm hand on the bridle. He knew again the sensation, like nothing else in the world, of being one with great sinews, of terrific power for speed, which comes to the man who rides a great horse and loves that horse.

The plains flew backward under the mare's heels in a steady canter that needed no stops for breathing, but the sun was red above the horizon before the smudge of smoke above Grand Junction brushed the hilltop ahead. As if she knew her duty, the horse bounded up the incline with new vigor. The rough trace of a road which he followed became a concrete highway and he set the mare to a gallop along its margin. Abruptly, he hauled her up on her haunches, and she shied about while the Spider leaned from the saddle to confront the three men who had sprung from ambush. They held shotguns with their gaping black muzzles of death leveled on Wentworth....

"Now where might you be going, stranger?" drawled the leader, a weary-looking man in faded overalls. "Your hawss is downright lathered."

The Spider eyed the man suspiciously through a tense moment, saw honesty in the steady, blue eyes. "El Gaucho is going to raid Grand Junction as soon as the banks open," he said sharply, patting his restive mare's neck. "There was need to lather her."

The mare nickered and somehow the men drew nearer and looked at this dark-cloaked figure with more confidence. They knew and loved horses in this country. A man who loved his horse, and whose horse loved him....

"Who are you, stranger, and how come you know about the Gaucho?" the weary one asked. His whole appearance was dejected, even to the drooping of his sandy mustache, but the brightness of his eyes belied his manner.

Wentworth leaned on his saddle bow. "Where I come from, it isn't considered real bright to ask questions like that," he drawled. "Who are you?"

FOR A moment there was a sharpening of those steady, blue eyes, then the man laughed. "Reckon you're right. My monicker's Hart."

The Spider nodded. "I am Gaucho's enemy," he said grimly. "I just escaped from his camp. Will one of you gentlemen go with me to warn the town?"

Hart gazed at him, then disappeared into the bushes and returned with a buckskin horse that looked tough. He swung up easily. "You boys," he told his companions, "keep on watching here for this here Gaucho and dash back anyway, if you hear shooting."

The mare and the buckskin leveled out for the city, hoofs flying. Wentworth shouted a question above the whip of the wind, but the answer disappointed him. He had hoped the men in the shrubbery were outposts on guard against El Gaucho, but they were merely a posse hunting a thief. The Spider's mouth shut more grimly at the news. That meant no preparations had been made for the battle to come…. Hart was sheriff, Wentworth gathered. That would help some in speeding the assembly of a defense force.

Finally the first scattered houses of the town began to flash past. Their horses' hooves were beating on pavement. Hart raised a voice that had shrill carrying power.

"El Gaucho is coming! To the town hall! Bring your guns!"

Over and over, he shouted that warning as he raced. Before the two on horseback had passed from sight, men and women were running into the streets, carrying rifles, strapping revolvers to their thighs. It had not been a full generation since these people had harked to other cries of alarm that were almost as terrible. Wentworth and Hart might have been men in doeskins with long rifles across their saddles. "To the blockhouse! The Indians are coming!"

Wentworth's eyes shot all about him, surveying the town in the early morning light. To the west flowed a shallow stream whose banks were cut steep by erosion. A bridge.... That would be easily guarded. The Gaucho would hardly attack from that direction. To the south, where the main highway led out, was broken terrain, but to reach that, El Gaucho's raiders would have to circle the entire town. Still it must be either from that direction or East. The Spider had come from the north without sighting the killer's cohorts.

The town was narrow, strung out along the river bank, and it seemed certain El Gaucho would seek to enter from the side so as to travel through as little hostile territory as possible. A smoldering anger had possession of Wentworth now as he glanced over the fleeing people. So many of these neat white-painted homes would be destroyed in the battle to come. Too many of them were frame. They would scarcely resist rifle bullets, and flames would play havoc.

In the small, grassy plot before the old town hall, which was built of red brick and topped with a belled cupola, Hart flung himself from his horse and dashed inside the building. Seconds later, the bell began an excited, bellowing clangor. People stopped in the streets to stare, automobiles spun to the curb. Wentworth sat his horse before the old steps of the building and threw his arms high above his head, gesturing to everyone in sight. When Hart came out again, his gun in plain evidence on his thigh and a rifle in the crook of his elbow, there was a growing crowd and, moment by moment, other men came. The ranks bristled with the barrels of rifles.

Hart glanced at Wentworth, sitting calmly erect on his lathered horse, his head thrown back, the cape draped in almost military style from his shoulders.

"Tell them about it, stranger," he ordered calmly.

WENTWORTH NODDED. The sheriff was a shrewd man. He knew that the startling words that were to be pronounced would gain more credence, swifter action, from the Spider because of his dramatic appearance—since Hart supported what he said. The Spider's calculating gray-blue eyes swept the crowd. Men were here who had fought before, grim-faced, eyes narrowed from the hot sun of the plains. Wentworth felt a growing sense of satisfaction. He was glad that the first organized stand against El Gaucho was to be made by men like these.

He lifted a slow hand toward the sun and there was an instant, waiting silence among the thousand men who had gathered before him.

"El Gaucho is coming to destroy Grand Junction," Wentworth said, his voice deep and strong. He paused then, saw the faces before him grow hard and determined. It pleased him. "I was their prisoner and escaped to bring you the warning. Do I need to tell you what El Gaucho's men will do if they are allowed to enter?"

A rumbling voice of anger answered him, the cry of bitter men. Wentworth turned to Hart. "I have some plans for defense," he said. "Shall I…?"

"Go ahead," Hart nodded. "I'll check."

Wentworth smiled grimly. Hart thought he was all right, but he was giving notice that he'd keep an eye on the proceedings. The Spider turned to the crowd again, studied faces. He knew men. His life had often depended on the faculty for reading men's character at a glance. He had been a soldier.…He leveled a hand pointing to a middle-aged man with a square, heavy face.

"Pick out ten men and ambush the south entrance of the highway," he said. "If you lack arms, commandeer them from stores. If El Gaucho's men come by automobile, remember a wrecked car will disable more men than a dead occupant of the car." Hart cut in: "Go to it, Johnson."

Johnson pivoted and began picking men from the crowd about him. Wentworth sent another similar squad to the northern entry, to the bridge; sent fifty men to cover the eastern fringe of the town where there was no road. Twenty were sent to barricade each of the town's three banks. Autos were to blockade every street that led to a bank.

"As much as possible," Wentworth said sharply, "get all

women and children into the town hall and other stone or brick buildings. El Gaucho will use fire and his men are beasts."

At the town hall, which was pretty much the center of the place, a force of three hundred men was assembled, roughly divided into six companies. There were ranks of automobiles parked before the building for quick action. Those who could not pile into the cars would go on foot. When these arrangements had been made, Wentworth and Hart stood quietly together on the steps of the Town Hall with the men who would head the companies. Hart had a machine gun in his hands. Wentworth would depend upon his automatics and revolvers for which he got a supply of extra ammunition. He felt a hard readiness in all his body for the battle. If it were well fought, they might be able to turn back El Gaucho and damage the morale of his men. It would take a good many tortures to stiffen their backbone for a new assault. The difficulty of the defense lay in the shortage of rifles and of ammunition. The supplies of the stores had soon been exhausted. They provided enough for about two hours of hard fighting if men conserved their shots. But El Gaucho would have machine guns. He had entire squads armed with portable rapid-fire weapons stolen from police arsenals in some of his raids. He would have grenades and tear-gas bombs....

Wentworth glanced at his watch. A quarter past nine. The assault would begin any moment. The men about him moved restlessly, peering off toward the streets and the ranks of automobiles. A steady procession of women and children hurried, many weeping, into the town hall which already was jammed to overflowing. Ten minutes ticked past and nothing happened.

The Spider's eyes quested over the city, stopped abruptly as they caught a smudge of greenish smoke. His gaze narrowed, and he turned toward Hart.

"I don't think there's any doubt El Gaucho has been warned that we are ready for him," he said quietly, "but that won't turn him back. Do you know of any reason, Hart, why that man's chimney over there would be sending out *green* smoke?"

Hart gazed where Wentworth indicated and a harsh curse rasped from his throat. He took a quick step forward, then checked. He said, "Why, damn it, stranger, that's *my* house…. But there ain't any fire in my furnace. Or there wasn't when I left. I…!"

HIS VOICE choked off as a ragged burst of firing ripped out to the south and, almost simultaneously, at the north end of town. The group of men on the steps of the town hall stiffened. A few started toward their companies.

"Wait," Wentworth rasped shortly. "Wait for motorcycle couriers."

The firing continued. Machine guns took up their sharp, throaty chattering. There was the thudding rumble of a grenade. Hart stood, stony-faced, eyes hot with rage. "Look, Hart," a man said to him. "Johnson is going to be wiped out if we don't…."

A motorcycle roared up the street, bumped the curb and chattered straight up to the steps. The rider flung off and ran up to Hart.

"Five cars tried to crash through at the south end," he panted. "Johnson stopped three, but the other two got past. He's got three men left."

"Ten more men ought to take care of those two cars," Wentworth said. Hart nodded, though his face was pale with the knowledge that seven defenders had fallen. He jerked out an order to the head of one of the companies. The man raced forward and his voice reached ahead of him. Ten men detached themselves from one of the huddled groups and went toward cars. The other men were dead quiet, waiting. Off to the north, the shooting had stopped entirely and no courier appeared. A full company was sent in that direction, scattered over four different streets, keeping close to buildings, hunting cover.

Hart turned, thin-lipped, to Wentworth. "It's the east all right," he said flatly. "Two companies ought to back up the fifty men we sent over there."

Wentworth nodded agreement. "If you'll stay here with the other three companies in reserve," he said, "I'll go to the east. But, Hart, I'm after just one thing… I'm going to kill El Gaucho!"

Hart held out his hand. "Good luck, stranger. None of us will ever forget this."

Wentworth's lips were tight against his teeth, but his grip of Hart's hand was firm and solid. "Good luck!"

Hart nodded. "Good luck… Spider!"

HIS LAST word was no more than a movement of lips, an almost soundless whisper. Wentworth's hand tightened upon his a bit more. Then he was gone, springing to the saddle of Carollotta's mare. He paused for a brief moment before the two companies nearest the eastern end of the town hall yard, looking at them slowly.

"The attack is on the east," he said, making his voice carry to them all easily. "These two companies are going there before it begins. You will be outnumbered and outarmed, but you will fight from cover… and you are fighting for your homes and your wives and sweethearts!"

A rumble of anger ran over the men. Their hands upon their guns were white with tension.

"You are brave," Wentworth said flatly, "but don't be foolish. Hide as well as you can; keep to cover. *Don't* be brave. Be stubborn. Don't give way, but don't show yourselves. Machine gunners are not brave, just deadly. And, one last word—" He paused, and held them with his silence, every eye centered on him—"Don't let one of your women fall into their hands. It would be kinder to—kill the women! These men of El Gaucho are the renegades of the border, the wolves of the cities. That's all!"

He saluted the two captains. "Carry on," he said shortly, then he spun his horse in a *demi-volte* and sent her thudding across the grass. She took the chain railing in an easy spring and was racing down the street. Before he had gone a block, he heard ahead of him to the eastward a ragged burst of firing that was heavier and more vicious than any that had broken out before. A half-dozen machine guns began to splutter. Bombs sent their rumbling thunder across the town. Then came a sound that brought a cry to Wentworth's lips, drew him far forward on the neck of his horse with the urgency for greater speed.

Field artillery had opened fire!

146

CHAPTER 12
EL GAUCHO STRIKES

EVEN AS he dashed to bolster the courage of the defenders, Wentworth saw the roof and the wall of a house lift before the blast of a screaming shell and collapse in debris. Three men were huddled in the ruins, dead. Down the length of the street, he could see a ragged line of soldiers in red advancing with the motley mob of El Gaucho's killers behind them. Some of the red men were falling, but the others came on unwavering.

Lead began to sing viciously past Wentworth's ears. He swung into a side street, picketed his horse and rushed forward on foot, keeping close to the walls until he was within a block of the outer rim of houses. Three shells in quick succession landed among the buildings ahead. One house lifted, fell in upon itself. Another had a gaping hole torn in its side and over the ruins, smoke… then red tongues of fire, began to creep.

He saw a dozen of the defenders flee backward from the front line and he called to them.

"More troops are coming," he shouted, "rally here!"

He got the twelve together in a side street, sent one back as a courier, with orders for the two companies that were coming to line both sides of three parallel streets to take cover inside of buildings, especially in cellars. The eleven men who remained he posted at opposite corners of the side streets. They caught up debris from a shell-wrecked house, hurriedly erected barricades, threw mattresses and pieces of furniture down as shields.

The soldiers of El Gaucho were still yards away and Wentworth left the men at work, preparing to enfilade the attackers while he rushed on to build a similar defense at the next corner, leaving orders to fire three rounds, then retreat through the trap that was being laid by the two supporting companies.

At each corner, parallel to the line of attack, he set up barricades in side streets. Two of them were weakly manned by four men and it was with these that Wentworth stayed, waiting for the attack. The field pieces, of which Wentworth figured there were three, had ceased firing with the breaking of resistance along the outer edge of the town. Now the soldiers of El Gaucho were advancing double-quick time.

Wentworth looked at the grim faces of the men about him. They would die rather than retreat, Wentworth knew. He ordered them to hold their fire when the first of the attackers came in sight, advancing cautiously with bayonets on their rifles. With them sauntered El Gaucho's lieutenant, De Moltkez, without a weapon in his hand, although there was a sword at his side, and an automatic in its holster. The Spider's automatic came into his palm without conscious thought, but he, too, held his fire, waiting.

A feeble, feeble force, these four men with him! Two behind the barricade across the street, two here with him. But they were well protected. Wentworth lifted his automatic as the soldiers came warily forward. Scarcely thirty feet away now. Aiming at De Moltkez's stomach, Wentworth squeezed the trigger, signaling a volley at the same time.

Four rifles crashed with his automatic and four men went down with De Moltkez. The four soldiers lay where they had fallen, but De Moltkez stumbled to his feet. His sword rasped from its scabbard and he hailed those in the rear.

"Forward!" he shouted. "Forward!"

Wentworth's lips felt cold and hard. His eyes burned. He knew the meaning of that failure to kill. The man wore armor beneath his uniform. And now, as he stood facing the rear, his spiked helmet protected his head and the back of his neck. Wentworth aimed deliberately at the hand that held the sword, shattered it with a swift shot.

THE SWORD fell; De Moltkez's arm flung down with the impact of the lead. He continued to order his men on, and the Spider felt a momentary glow of admiration. Courage was a rare and priceless thing and, though this man's cause was an evil, a murderous one, it was impossible not to respect a brave enemy. Wentworth put a bullet through De Moltkez's leg, saw him fall, saw soldiers cluster about him.

The four rifles were taking heavy toll among the thick press of red men who continued to crowd forward, but the answering hail of lead was a hot breath of death. One of the riflemen with Wentworth surged to his feet with a slug through his head and pitched forward over the barricade. With the second, Wentworth sprang into the house beside them, raced through it to the backyard and climbed fences along the block to safety. On the next corner, they took a new stand. He caught a low cry, whirled to see a man signal from a window. The captain of one of the supporting companies was in the basement of a house directly opposite!

Wentworth raced to him. "Hold fire until they fill the entire distance you have men posted, then mow them down," he ordered rapidly. "We'll lead them…!"

The thud of a bullet, the sigh of the rifleman with him interrupted Wentworth, the man collapsed against him, dying. A curse was torn from the captain's throat.

"Jack," he said hoarsely. "Damn them to hell! They killed Jack!"

Wentworth crouched against the side of the house, his two automatics speaking in slow rhythm. His marksmanship was the product of endless hours of practice; the guns were like parts of his own body. When he shot, a man fell. During that long minute, the bodies of the dead checked further advance. He turned back to the captain, saw tears streaming down his white face.

"He was my brother," the company leader said.

Wentworth pointed down the street, his own face drawn and pale.

"There are the men who killed him," he announced flatly. "Wait until there are many in your trap!"

He retreated, dodging from doorway to doorway, reloading his automatic as he went. This defense was costing a terrific number of casualties, but El Gaucho was taking even heavier losses. This would be a costly raid for him.

Wentworth's continued escape from harm was a seeming miracle, but actually it was caution and experience. Men had gone through two and three years of the World War, through countless bitter battles, without a wound. They were those who knew how to take advantage of every bit of cover—who kept their eyes and their guns on the enemy every second. A man who was quick with his guns had an armor in his bullets.

But the Spider felt that he had done all he could here. The soldiers already were marching double quick time into the trap. It was useless to expose himself further. The Spider must live—to kill El Gaucho! Wentworth became aware, now that the pressure of close attack was fading with his retreat, that heavy firing was going on in the center of the city. From the sound, Hart's three companies must be bitterly engaged also.

Wentworth recovered his picketed horse, raced toward the town hall. His eyes flicked the skyline. Black smoke and flames were tonguing up in a dozen places and the scream of shells shrilled overhead, echoed by the bellowing thunder of their explosions. There were other, less pleasant sounds. Now and then, the scream of a woman arose.

Curses squeezed out between Wentworth's teeth. Those renegades of El Gaucho! He suspected that the bandit king encouraged bestiality to spread the terror of his advance. As he raced past a side street, he saw a girl fleeing from a man—and losing the race. Wentworth reined his horse back on its haunches, pivoted back to the street corner. His automatic spoke once and the man twisted backward violently, rolled over twice before he lay, limp in death, in the dusty street.

THE GIRL looked up with a startled, white face, then dodged into a house. Wentworth swore as he swung the horse about again. Of what use to save one woman when all over the city…? The mare was stretched out like an arrow, head thrust forward, tail flying out straight behind. Her rhythmic gait was a song of power. Wentworth patted her neck as he raced on. A brave little beast. After her rest, she was as fresh and strong as ever....

The town hall square was deserted when he smashed out into the open from a side street. He pulled the mare up, rearing, to peer about. Dead men lay like abandoned bundles of clothing about the street. The bank across the street was shattered by explosions, its windows blank gaping holes, its barricades breached by grenade craters. What, was it all in vain then? Had El Gaucho swept in from some other direction while his men had fought a futile skirmish there on the east?

But the firing was still heavy up the street there. A tight group of men broke out of the opposite side of the square, coming at a hard run. The square-built Johnson was in their lead, eight men behind him. At sight of Wentworth, they swerved in his direction and he sent the mare to meet them.

"We cleaned them up on the South," Johnson rasped. There was a blood stain on his shoulder, a jagged rip across his temple. His hat was gone, but his thick, brown hand was steady on the butt of his revolver.

"I think they're stopped on the east, too," Wentworth said. "I got one of their leaders and they were walking into a trap of a hundred rifles."

Johnson looked about him haggardly. "God, they're dead here, too," he said dully. "I lost thirteen men."

Wentworth looked over the squad behind the man. They were white-faced, but their anger was a hard, enduring thing. He nodded. "I'll see what's happening up the street here," he said. "You follow, but keep to cover."

He dashed forward, hearing still the battering of the three field pieces off there to the east, hearing the crashing of volley fire where the soldiers in red walked into ambush. Dropping from the horse at a run, he peered about the corner.

From the cover of surrounding buildings, fully fifty of El Gaucho's renegades were pumping lead, hurling grenades at a bank building that was being stubbornly defended. Even as he looked, a group of bandits burst from cover and went forward with bayonets fixed.

Wentworth threw up an arm in urgent signal to the nine behind him and, dropping prone on the ground, opened fire with both automatics. His guns bellowed death. Johnson's voice was breathless, but sharp in command, and Wentworth heard his men hit the ground, heard their rifles blasting about him.

Almost before their flanking fire had begun, the charge was broken, and a dozen men lay dead on the ground outside the barricade. From the bank, a cheer went up and redoubled fire blasted from its windows and fortified door. Wentworth drew his little command back to cover just in time as machine-gun lead hurricaned up the street.

He led his small squad in a rapid sweep around the block. While El Gaucho's men still scoured their first position with lead, they reached a second street that opened on their flanks. A dozen bandits were in sight, behind posts and automobiles. Before they were aware of their new peril, the rifles of Johnson's men opened again and death was among them.

The firing to eastward was dwindling now and Wentworth detached a man to summon reinforcements from the ambushing companies. Once more, he executed a circling movement, but this time the enemy was prepared and two of Wentworth's little command went down. The squad kept moving anyway. There was no danger of a frontal attack because of covering fire from the bank's barricades, but they were open to a flanking assault. WENTWORTH TURNED over his command to the competent, grim-faced Johnson, and galloped on through the streets of the town. He had failed to sight El Gaucho here, and that was his chief concern. Whirling to the left, to intercept the northern highway which stretched toward the plains encampment of El Gaucho, Wentworth met sentry lines. He dropped two men whose rifles were too slow and whirled back. In an alleyway, he left the mare again and went through backyards toward the highway again. There, if anywhere, El Gaucho would pass.

The Spider, creeping along fences toward a position that would command the highway, felt a new respect for El Gaucho. The man was a skillful strategist. If he failed, it was because of the inefficiency of his lieutenants. He had posted men to protect his line of retreat through a city that would be full of his enemies. But not all were enemies, Wentworth recalled. Someone had signaled that the town was prepared for defense—the green smoke from the sheriff's house.

Also there had been, along the streets he had covered, certain homes which apparently were immune to attack, their windows were whole, their doors unshattered by marauding men. Possibly they were allies of El Gaucho! Wentworth felt the tension of anger creeping into his muscles. It was damnable to think that anyone should ally himself with such a criminal, but it gave new proof of the man's power.

The house toward which Wentworth worked his way was darkly shuttered and apparently deserted. It had the look of those other places that he had seen, which he suspected of being those of El Gaucho sympathizers. There was a certain grim set to his lips as he stole forward, an implacable coldness in his eyes. An abrupt thought struck him that this house must be near where the green smoke had arisen....

A cellar window yielded silently to his shrewd manipulations and he slipped across the dark basement toward stairs which he could dimly discern on its opposite side. Nothing hindered him as he went through the kitchen toward the front hall.... He froze in the shadow of the stairs that led upward. Soft footsteps creaked across the floor over his head.

Cautiously, the Spider slid up the stairs. The footsteps were still now. With their ceasing, a throbbing silence filled the house, as if the building itself were waiting. For what?

Wentworth frowned at the whisper of his nerves; his mind, which was recalling what had happened when before he ignored that warning of his subconscious mind. He knew suddenly that danger was here! The certainty stopped him halfway up the stair. He drew out his sword, clamping the blade between his fingers to prevent sound.

Out in the street, a woman screamed and a gale of ribald laughter followed. A volley of rifle fire crackled in the distance. On the floor below the Spider, a mouse squeaked and scampered across bare wood with a faint scratching noise. Presently,

Wentworth became aware of movement above him again, dim creaking of boards beneath unwary feet. Someone was shifting his weight. Wentworth looked upward along his sword blade and saw a man's hair edge over the bannister, followed by two inches of forehead, then the eyes....

Wentworth jabbed with his sword, held its point within a half-inch of the eyes.

"Stand up!" he ordered softly.

The eyes widened and, as the sword advanced, a man raised his body.

"I have an automatic in my left hand," Wentworth cautioned. "If you should try to shoot, you would be dead before you could wink. Now, walk to the head of the steps with me."

THE MAN had not opened his lips. He walked along the railing as Wentworth climbed the stairs. The gun in his right hand hung limply, and he made no resistance when it was taken.

"What kind of mercuric compound did you use to make the green smoke?" asked the Spider softly.

A quiver ran over the man's face, a flaccid weakening of his jaw, a quiver of his eyelids. Wentworth cursed. He dropped guns and sword, caught the man's shirt with his left hand and hit him twice with his fist, let the man slump to the floor. He stooped and bound him rapidly with his own belt, tied his shoe laces together, then wrote rapidly on a card, using his left hand, sealed what he had written with the emblem of the Spider. When he left, he would deposit this gentleman where he could be found. Sheriff Hart would do the rest to the man who had signaled to the enemy with the green smoke. His guilt was unquestionable.

The Spider slipped to the front of the house and peered out between the slats of the closed blinds. The laughter and the screams still sounded there, and now he saw the reason. Soldiers and gangsters of El Gaucho lined the street. About ten of them were in sight and Wentworth knew from their spacing that the guard extended that way from the center of the town to its outskirts. Between the lines of men were three girls, hysterical with fear, trying frantically to escape their tormentors. Each time they dashed toward the lines, a soldier would seize them and rip off another bit of their clothing. One girl was already entirely nude. Whenever a girl crouched to the earth, seeking to escape further torment, a bullet would scorch the ground near her. Once more the Spider's guns leaped to his hands, but he stayed the shot, looked rapidly about. The room was a sleeping chamber and he crossed to the bed in a long bound, snatched up a pillow, then darted back to the window.

When next a soldier caught a girl, Wentworth pressed the muzzle of his automatic deep into the pillow and fired. His aim was instinctive, never-failing, like the aim of a baseball pitcher. The soldier reeled backward and the girl broke through the line and escaped into an alleyway. The muffled cough of the automatic was not noticed, hut the soldier lay on his back with a bullet through his forehead. No man left his post, but there was a panic stiffness among them that betrayed their sudden terror. Their eyes desperately searched the houses about them. A grim smile touched the Spider's lips as the other two girls stole away unnoticed. If only El Gaucho would betray himself to his guns in the same way....

Wentworth settled down to wait. The soldiers took no action, but they indulged in no more ribaldry. Death hovered over their heads. The minutes dragged past. One automobile roared up the street, but Wentworth was confident it did not contain El Gaucho, for the soldiers made no move to salute. El Gaucho would not have permitted such a laxness even in the midst of battle. Sounds of the fight still drifted downwind from the center of the town and a great restlessness seized Wentworth. Had he been too confident of victory?

He took short turns up and down before the window, went back to inspect his prisoner, who had recovered consciousness. Wentworth gazed down into his fear-stricken face. This man was responsible for many deaths this day. If El Gaucho had not been warned, he might have attempted the raid without strategy and been wiped out by an unexpected ambush. The supine man quailed beneath the Spider's blazing glare.

ABRUPTLY, WENTWORTH jerked him to his feet. Deliberately, he removed his own belt and made a noose which he fitted about the man's throat. He then fastened its end over a hook so that the man was pulled upon his tiptoes. In that position, he could manage to keep himself from strangling, but if he sagged to his heels…. Wentworth stalked back to the window.

"For God's sake," the man begged, "don't leave me like this! I'll… I'll choke to death!" His voice came pitifully to Wentworth. Once, his words were strangled in his throat when he sagged with the noose. When that had happened three times, Wentworth returned to confront him.

"For God's sake," the man pleaded hoarsely. "Let me go. I'll… I'll do anything you say, but please…."

Wentworth appeared to consider while the man dropped once more into the noose. His face turned blue with congested blood and his eyes bulged before he could balance himself again on his toes.

"You couldn't do anything that would be worth saving your life," said the Spider skeptically, but there was a hard, swift eagerness in his heart. It was barely possible the prisoner had information of importance. That was the hope behind his torture.

"I have information about El Gaucho," the man whispered hoarsely.

The Spider looked dubious. "If it's good enough…."

"I know the next town he's going to raid," the man panted. "It's Jamesville, Indiana."

"When?"

"Day after tomorrow."

"Is that all?"

The man tried to get his shoulders against the wall to help support himself, but the belt was too short. He gagged. "I'm supposed to go ahead and warn him if they know about it, as I did here, I… I could give him the wrong signal."

Wentworth learned that the favorable signal was red smoke, then he released the man from his strangling belt, locked him in the closet and went back to the window. The soldiers stood at present arms, a salute! The Spider's teeth showed between tight lips and he weighed his automatic in his hand. But even as his hopes of killing El Gaucho rose, the soldiers grounded their arms again and began hopping to the running board of automobiles that stopped to take them on.

A jagged curse ripped from Wentworth's lips. He knew what that meant. El Gaucho already had passed! While the Spider had been busy with his prisoner, the leader himself had gone by within reach of his guns! Deliberately, savagely, Wentworth opened fire on the autos that were speeding the soldiers away. His shots ticked off as regularly as a clock's balance wheel. And each bullet pierced a gasoline tank. Pursuers would overtake many bandits this day....

When the last of the automobiles had sped past, Wentworth caught up his prisoner and, with the man on his shoulder, ran from the house. He deposited the man in the middle of the highway, then hastened to his picketed horse. Moments later, he was sending the valiant mare out into the plains, racing, racing back to the encampment of El Gaucho. He had a twofold purpose: Death and life; justice against El Gaucho, rescue for Tom Barker!

CHAPTER 13
THREAT OF DISASTER

IT WAS a weary ride back to the encampment of El Gaucho, horse and rider jaded from hours of violent activity. Wentworth had had no sleep since his few hours on the plane flying westward and before that.... His mind felt numbed, but there could be no rest. The Spider was confident that, after the costly partial defeat at Grand Junction, El Gaucho would not dare to continue his encampment. If he left there, Wentworth would have no clue to his whereabouts prior to the promised attack upon Jamesville, Indiana. Even that might have been a lie told by the prisoner to save his life. And by that time, Barker might be slain.

Wentworth thus spurred himself as the horse drummed out the long miles, stirred his wearied body to new efforts. His thoughts turned inward. A smile that was strange to the harsh face of the Spider touched his lips. At least, Nita's fears would have been relieved by now. The telegraph wires must be humming with the news of the battle at Grand Junction and, if Sheriff Hart did not reveal his guess of Wentworth's identity as the Spider, at least there would be accounts of a stranger in a black cape who brought the warning. Yes, Nita would know he was safe.

Safe! The word mocked him. Safe for a while, yes, escaped from the immediate threat of El Gaucho's torture, but speeding back as rapidly as possible to new encounters. El Gaucho was a graver menace than he had believed possible. Already the tentacles of criminal organization were reaching out beyond the man's immediate following. World dominion was his crazy dream. He would never attain that, but in the process of his efforts, he could destroy thousands of lives and lay a hundred cities waste....

Dusk was crawling up the slope of the rounded hill when at last Wentworth reached the brink of the sunken plateau where El Gaucho had his encampment. He stopped the weary mare short of the crest and crawled the last fifteen feet on his belly. When, at last, he could look down into the valley, a great shout of anger rose in his throat. He sprang to his feet, ran back to the mare, raced her headlong down the slope. There was not a tent in the valley, not a trace of its former occupation except the refuse of an encampment. But there was a single light burning in a room of the mansion El Gaucho had used as headquarters. Could it be possible that the man was still there? Wentworth weighed hope against hope.

He knew when he was fifty yards away from the building that his hope was vain. There was no automobile in front and even the garden had a stripped and deserted aspect. Wentworth pulled down the nearly exhausted mare to a walk, finally halted within twenty feet of the window from which the light came. It was the room where, the night before, he had talked with Carollotta, and made her a promise that he would return.

With the thought, he threw himself from the horse's back and strode toward the window. He was suddenly strong with hope again. He had promised he would return, and the girl had been forced to leave before that time. She had left a light burning, unnoticeable in daytime, but a guiding star at night. There would be a note inside, a message from Carollotta. Wentworth was abruptly positive of that. He heard the mare nicker, then her feet clopped rapidly away. He spun about, but she was only going toward the stable from which he had taken her at dawn. He smiled after the hungry mare, then caught the sill and muscled himself upward....

A sudden gust of irresistible wind pinned him against the side of the house. His hat was blown through the window and smashed glass rained down upon his head. His eardrums felt burst. Half dazed, he dropped to the ground and turned toward the stable. The building was gone, blown to bits, and of the mare there was nothing at all to be seen. Wentworth leaned his shoulders against the wall, breathing heavily, almost sobbingly. His concussion-numbed mind groped its way to the answer. A bomb planted in the stable—a trap! For himself? He shook his head. It must be it was intended, then, for the pursuers. By the heavens, El Gaucho planned well!

THERE COULD be no doubt that the camp had been evacuated before El Gaucho attacked Grand Junction. These mines—there would be others—had been planted in the hope of destroying those who came here at the bidding of his escaped prisoner.

Wentworth turned back to the window, climbed in. There was grief in his heart for the mare, as at the loss of a personal friend. She had been faithful and greathearted, willing even in exhaustion…. He stooped slowly and picked up his hat, pulled it down over his head. The light—it was a lamp burning beside the bed. He lifted it, and under the base lay a folded piece of paper. Simple, that light signal, but effective. Carollotta had brains.

The note read:

"I believe you will come back for Tommy. El Gaucho is taking him with us, and I think he will surely die by the horses when there is time and a place for that. They all believe he is your servant and that you have left him behind to observe and in some way communicate with you. I don't know where we are going, except that it is toward the east. I heard them talking about New York, but I do not know if that is where we go. I will do what I can for Tommy, but my only weapon is that I know El Gaucho… too well!"

There was no greeting, no signature. Wentworth pulled his cigarette lighter from his pocket and touched flame to the paper, watched it burn to ashes which crushed to powder beneath his foot. He was frowning heavily, wishing that there had been something more definite that Carollotta might tell him… Suddenly he threw himself face down on the floor and rolled. When his shoulders hit the floor, his guns leaped to his hands and he fired. The man whose stealthy step he had heard in the hallway was hammered against the doorjamb and pivoted there, slowly, painfully, with both hands clutching the wood. His gun dropped where he fell, straight backward to the floor. His head bounced.

Wentworth got to his feet slowly, guns ready for further enemies. He fired twice through the doorway, skimming each doorpost at the height of a man's peeping head. But there was no indication of a hit. Nevertheless, as he walked forward, he kept his eyes on the shadows. For a moment, he had known poignant fear. It had flashed through his mind that the forces of Grand Junction might have arrived, and in the surprise, he had killed a man of the law. And the Spider would take a wound himself, even a mortal injury, rather than fire on the police or any of their allies. But a glance at the victim of his lead dispelled his apprehension. His was the face of the criminal, vicious and cruel.

Wentworth bent slowly over him, frowning at an armband insignia on his arm, the colors of El Gaucho's pennant, a purple and a scarlet stripe. As he bowed, he heard stealthy movement in the hallway, but even as he pulled up his head it was too late. He saw a lithe body springing through the air, the gleam of a drawn knife… Wentworth threw himself aside to avoid the violent downstroke of the blade. He dodged that, but impact hurled him to the floor.

There was a moment of desperate scramble. The knife nicked the Spider's ear, crunched into the floor. The moment's delay while his assailant dislodged it was all that Wentworth needed. His hands shot up and closed crushingly about the man's throat. He wrenched, rolled and threw his body straight forward in a somersault, while his hands kept close hold on the neck of the other. His thumbs were locked beneath the chin, his fingers biting into the vertebrae at the back. When he came down, all the weight of his body would be in the wrench upon the spine. A broken neck….

THEN, IN the midst of the movement, Wentworth got a glimpse of the face of his attacker. Tousled, brown hair straggled over his forehead and the eyes were deep blue, bulging now with the throttling fingers at his throat, the teeth were bared by drawn-back lips. Wentworth had a flashing thought that the boy beneath him was Tommy Barker. He was no more than a kid, eighteen or nineteen… The glimpse was enough to loosen Wentworth's fingers. He somersaulted, came to his feet and spun about to face his antagonist.

The boy lay flat on his back, his right hand drawn up against his body. As Wentworth stared, the hand came limply loose and revealed the hilt of the knife driven deep into his side. The wrench of the throw Wentworth had contrived had turned the knife on its wielder. The Spider came slowly close to him, frowning, his eyes dark. The lad had a wild, willful face, but there was no viciousness here, none of the criminal taint.

"You got me... Spider," the boy gasped. "You're... pretty good."

Wentworth went down on one knee beside him, but he did not look at the wound. He already knew there was nothing he could do to save him. He brushed the hair back from the boy's forehead and a bitter inward grief twisted him, a grief strangely mixed with rage. This boy might have made a splendid man. There was strength and courage in his face. And, because of El Gaucho, he lay here dying.

"I thought I'd play smart," the boy panted. "Said Joe couldn't take you... with guns. Said I'd get you when... he was dead. It's other way 'round, Spider... ain't it?"

Wentworth's lips were twisted. "No use kidding you, son," he said. "You're right."

Dark fear sprang into the boy's blue eyes, his lips quivered, then set. "I don't feel no pain yet," he whispered. "Gee, this is going to be... tough on ma. There's seven younger than me. And Earl... got hisself killed... just like I did. Playing fool."

Wentworth was shaken. Death he had seen a thousand times, but this boy was so young! His youth cried up from the softness of his relaxed mouth, from the gangling long body of him. Wentworth drew out his handkerchief and wiped off the cold perspiration that stood out suddenly on the boy's forehead. He swallowed twice before he could speak.

"Listen, son," he said slowly, his compassion in his voice. "I'm damned sorry this had to happen." It was not Wentworth speaking, though he sometimes hated his dual nature. It was his other self, the Spider, telling him that perhaps something valuable could be learned from this dying member of El Gaucho's band... The kid was whispering....

"Gaucho paid me a hundred a month and a bonus when he fought... Geewhil—whilikins, I'd a gone to hell for that…!" The boy laughed and a bloody froth came to his lips for the Spider to sponge away. "Reckon I'm going there... fast. But mom has the farm paid for now."

The Spider it was who bent above the boy now. "Son," he said, "if you will tell me all you know, I'll see that your mother gets a hundred dollars a month for the rest of her life. I'll set up a trust fund."

The eyes of man and boy met, and those of the younger seemed very old. Pain was in them, pain and fear and now suspicion joined those, too. A spasm quivered over his gangling body, the eyes closed and his breath came, sharp and quick, through his mouth.

With his eyes closed, he whispered, "Swear it, Spider? They say... you always... keep your word."

Wentworth said heavily, "I swear."

The whispering went on for a long time, longer than Wentworth would have believed life could remain in that thin, battered body. When it was all done, the boy's eyes seemed luminous and large and his breathing was a heavy labor.

"Take care of ma," he breathed, "or I'll… h'ant you shore!"

WENTWORTH SMILED and it was not the smile of the Spider, but of the human, sympathetic man whose altruism had brought that dread killer of the night into being. He held out his hand.

"Shake, son," he said, "you're a real man. I'm… I'm sorry as hell about this."

The boy's lips moved faintly. It might have been a smile. His hand lay limp and cold within Wentworth's. He said, "Nuts to you."

A shudder swept him, and the labor of his breathing no longer tortured him. Wentworth touched the eyelids and pressed them shut. He stood through a long minute staring down at the boy's still form. Then he straightened with a wide movement of his shoulders as if he adjusted them to an old and heavy burden. He strode across the room to the window and was gone.

He went across-country to the spot the boy had indicated, found two horses tethered there. Then he rode down the valley toward the highway that led from Grand Junction. The sky was black as his cape, but spangled with stars. The moon pushed an orange rim above the valley's rim. He had fought off the depression that had held him there beside the dying boy, thrust such thoughts from his mind. What he had learned would send him as swiftly as planes could carry him to New York, but first he must wait to warn the troops which would presently come here that the buildings in the valley were all mined.

Leading the second horse, the Spider reached presently a point at the valley's end where he could mount a ridge above the dusty track that trailed beside the creek. There he dismounted and squatted on his heels to wait. The boy had said that New York, not Jamesville, was the next objective of El Gaucho. That meant that he had joined forces with Peterson, that all the nation's Underworld would be with him. Only loosely affiliated at first, of course, but El Gaucho, if he were allowed to continue, would soon tighten and strengthen the alliance.

After the disaster of Grand Junction, El Gaucho had separated his forces. Hereafter, they would never be assembled in one unit except at the scene of his crimes. Scattered into small bands, not wearing uniforms, they would travel as gypsies, as hoboes, as people touring in good cars, traveling in old cars and seeming to look for work; as work gangs going to seemingly authenticated places where factories awaited them.

The looting of the banks at the Junction had been part of a plan for financing these movements and preparing for greater victories to come. But that was not all. The Spider's discovery of sympathizers in Grand Junction had pointed to widespread affiliations and these were confirmed by the boy. These persons, highly paid, secretly opened banks, betrayed towns, gave information—some even contributed funds! There were thousands of dollars pouring in from such sources all the time, in addition to the tremendous loot.

El Gaucho had made, tentatively, a deal with Peterson, which had been confirmed from ten other cities besides New York, through the gang leaders, agreeing that the Underworld and political affiliations of those criminals should be thrown into the balance behind El Gaucho the moment that El Gaucho captured New York City!

The boy whispered that El Gaucho no longer had his eyes turned toward Bethania. Drunk with power, he proposed to take over the United States as his private kingdom! He had said, in a speech before his assembled myrmidons that, when the Underworld threw in with him, he would be proclaimed President! He intimated that members of Congress, high army and navy officials had been bought over. Ten days after that, the dying boy had whispered, El Gaucho promised that Washington would be in his power, and he would be installed in the White House itself!

TO WENTWORTH it sounded like the dream of an opium eater, but before this, fanatics who believed in themselves had seized control of a nation. There was no reason to believe that the United States could not be similarly conquered. There were enough self-seekers in the high places to make bribery possible. Yes, it was fantastic, but not as impossible as it sounded. The Spider could look with equanimity upon the boy's death now. No martyr's death had ever contributed more to a cause than this boy's mortal wound....

Only one other thing had the boy told Wentworth. El Gaucho had offered to pay its weight in gold to the man who obtained—*the Spider's head!*

It was bloodthirstily like El Gaucho to make such a proposition as that. He stipulated that the head itself must be brought to him to be weighed upon his scales and redeemed. Wentworth's face set grimly. He had had prices on his head before this. Fifty thousand dollars was standing against his name in a half dozen different rewards. But never before had so barbaric a proposal been made. He thought whimsically that his head was worth considerably more than its weight in gold to him—so long as it remained on his shoulders.

A whisper of hoofs on the sandy earth brought him to his feet, and he arose from where he had picketed the two horses below the crest of the ridge and climbed until he stood plainly in the moonlight—fifty yards from the long black line of horses that moved on toward El Gaucho's former encampment.

Wentworth sent a shrill cry toward the troops, then flaunted his cape against the night sky. "El Gaucho is gone!" he shouted. "But beware, there are bombs planted there. Beware! The Spider warns you!"

He repeated the message to make sure. He was understood, but as he spoke, he stepped slowly backward and with the last word, he leaped below the crest of the ridge. Seconds later, he vaulted to the saddle, ignoring the guns that had blasted up the slope toward him. The hoof beats of pursuers racketed up the slope, but it was slow work against sliding sand. When they reached the top, the Spider was a black figure speeding into the moon, with his cape flying backward from his shoulders.

Then, abruptly, the rider vanished, dipping into one of those numerous depressions which are scattered over the plains. But to those who watched from the ridge, it was as if he had leaped into the moon and disappeared, like a black-caped witch riding a broomstick. They looked at each other, and one man's hand rose surreptitiously to cross himself.

"The Spider!" he whispered.

CHAPTER 14
CITADEL OF CRIME

W HEN THE Spider reached Grand Junction again by a circuitous route, no one would have recognized him for the sinister being who, eight hours before, had led the people of the town into battle. The Spider's disguise had been destroyed, one of the many dead had supplied him with clothing, and his face was now that of Richard Wentworth.

It was a weary face, but it had a virility and a magnetism that drew the eyes of women and men, too. His entire body radiated strength, and despite his fatigue, there was a jaunty self-confidence about his shoulders, an arrogance in the poise of his head that would have marked him in any crowd.

Wentworth avoided any place where Sheriff Hart might be met, for Hart had heard the Spider use Wentworth's voice and his sudden memory of it might be fresh so soon after the happening. Wentworth visited a telegraph office first and sent two messages—one to Nita to say he was bound for New York; one to Jackson to bid him bring the Daimler to Newark airport. He made one more stop for clothing; then motored to the air field and chartered a plane to carry him eastward.

For a few minutes after the ship had lifted toward the sky, Wentworth sat watching the earth flow backward to the West, but his eyelids were weighted and presently, gratefully, he leaned his head back against the crash pad and slept, while the slipstream roared past his ears and the bellow of the engine beat on his brain. Nor did he awake until the slight jounce of the plane landing bounced his head against the pad. He opened his eyes then, saw Newark airport's hangars rushing toward him through the dusk. His sleep had rested him and he looked eagerly about for the Daimler, spotted its powerful bulk finally as the ship came to a stop and the pilot cut the engine.

It was Jackson, his stalwart shoulders set soldier-fashion, who came marching forward to greet him. He said only, "Good evening, major," but there was joy in his blue eyes. Jackson paid off the pilot while Wentworth hurried toward the car, his eyes peering vainly to penetrate its dark interior. He had not formulated any hope in his thoughts, but....

He opened the door and the dome light glowed softly in the tonneau. He stood gazing into the car. He did not speak. Nor did Nita van Sloan, who smiled gaily at him from the rear seat.

"You're an old meanie," said Nita. "You didn't tell me where you'd be landing, and I had to phone Jackson. Most humiliating, Mr. Wentworth. Most humiliating."

Wentworth got in slowly and closed the door. "You seem to bear up under the humiliation very well, Miss van Sloan," he whispered as he gathered her into his arms in the darkness that dropped as the door shut. Nita's hand clutched at his coat and she relaxed on his shoulder with a long shuddering sigh.

"Oh, Dick!" she whispered. "Oh, Dick!"

It was one of those precious moments snatched from eternity when these two who loved so greatly might surrender themselves to their love; when the anxieties of long days during which Death stalked them could be forgotten for a while. But it was over too soon. The gravity of the peril that hung over the nation could not be put aside, and Wentworth began to talk rapidly, telling all that he knew about El Gaucho's plans.

Nita told him then of her own stint, of the battle to rescue him, of Ram Singh's wounds, from which he was rapidly recovering.

"We've kept track of everyone we could," she said. "Peterson left town with you, but Yvonne is here." She gave Wentworth the address. "I'm sorry I misjudged Tommy Barker that way, but his actions were scarcely conducive to trust. Oh, let all that wait a little while, Dick. I have dinner prepared at home, a bottle of that excellent Chambertin from your own cellar...."

WENTWORTH SQUEEZED Nita's hand, weakening for the moment. Food? He had eaten hastily in Grand Junction before the take-off. Rest? He had slept in the plane. The laughter that came from his lips was not all pleasant.

"There is no time for it," he said shortly. "I haven't the slightest idea when the attack upon New York will be made. Any hour.... There's work for you, too, darling. See Commissioner Flynn. If Governor Kirkpatrick is in town, see him and tell them what I have told you tonight. Tell them I'll see them in the morning... with proof."

Nita made her voice cheerful. "You have this proof?"

"That's what I'm going for now," Wentworth said grimly. "I'll have to take this car, darling, for my disguise...."

Nita's hand touched his arm. "I knew it would be this way," she said without expression. "That's why I came to the field. Would you even have telephoned me, Dick?"

Wentworth's hand closed over hers. "No, darling," he said.

The Spider's sword spread into the man's mouth!

"You give me strength, dearest, but tonight I could be weak....
Forget it, sweetheart. Not many more days and we'll have El
Gaucho out of the running."

"And then there'll be another and another... and another."
Nita's voice was muffled, but the words came out with vehe-
mence, as if each one were alive and driving itself individually
from between her teeth. "Oh, Dick, will there never be an end?"

Wentworth sat rigidly beside her, hearing Nita voice the cry
that had risen in his own soul. They had thought the end was
near before El Gaucho had arisen... His hand, patting hers,
moved mechanically.

"Not tonight, sweetheart," he said huskily. "I..." He leaned
forward and rapped on the glass. "Get that taxi, Jackson."

Wentworth turned to Nita in the darkness and her arms
tightened about his shoulders. "Hurry, Dick," she whispered
against his mouth, "I'll be waiting. And forgive me. It's just that
sometimes...."

"I know! I know!" Wentworth pulled sharply away, descended
from the car to help Nita into the taxi, then sprang back into his
own car, threw Yvonne Musette's address at Jackson, and sank
back on the cushions. But the relaxation that usually he could
force upon himself—the one thing that enabled him to carry
on through months and years of ceaseless battle—had deserted
him. Black despair, an utter dejection had him by the throat. His
dauntless spirit quailed before the task before him, the power of
El Gaucho and his thousands.

Was he never, his traitor heart cried to him, to have the ordinary joys of life that other men knew? Was he always to duel

with death, to hear the vicious whine of bullets that just miss…
until some day one flew straight? For the moment, he hated the
thing he was, the Spider. It rebelled against the rigid discipline
of mind which could make him ruthless and nearly superhuman.
Of what good were all these things beside the sweets of a great
love that could never be? His human heart almost failed him, his
great will shaken by a burden almost too great for mortal to bear.

No one had ever seen Wentworth in one of these attacks of
black despair and he intended that no one ever should. That was
why he had thrust Nita brusquely from the car. The sweat beaded
his forehead and his hands, clenched and clenched again, were
cold and clammy. He was fighting a greater battle than even the
Spider's reckless dueling. He commanded his inner soul, the
core of indomitable strength that bore him through all trials,
and somewhere, somehow, that spirit answered. He dragged
out of his heart the superb fighting power—that unbreakable
will—which had carried him through many crises.

There was a moment when his hands shook, a moment when
his mouth was dry with the longing and the terror that gripped
him, then it was gone. As quickly as it had seized on him, the
depression vanished. Slowly, stiffly he turned his head and saw
that the car was near his goal. He gripped the speaking tube:

"Circle the park!"

HE LEANED out of the open window, breathed deep of
the aromatic odors of trees and banks of shrubs as the Daimler
purred along. Then he sank back into the car. His face slowly
became molded to a new sternness, a bitter power. He was…
the Spider!

His hands had never been surer nor swifter, the impersonation never more sinister. Wentworth's lips twisted a little as he saw the face of the Spider take form over his own in the brilliant light of the makeup table which was concealed with a wardrobe in the back of the Daimler's rear seat. The impersonation was good, but the pangs of its birth had been great.

It would be well, he considered, to carry his sword-cane tonight.... When the car stopped in the shadows of the trees and Jackson sprang to the pavement to throw open the door, Wentworth saw in his man's eyes the reflection of his own opinion. By the heavens! Jackson, accustomed as he was to this makeup, was startled and a little frightened at his appearance!

"Wait," Wentworth said simply. Then he slipped into the shadows and moved toward Yvonne's living quarters. This was, Wentworth knew, the most secret meeting place of the gangs whose loose confederation had practically ruled New York for ten years. Wentworth had nearly lost his life there once, when he had entered in disguise, and he knew something of its layout.

He entered through an iron grating opening beneath the front steps of the ancient brownstone house, which were preferred by many of the criminals since they were practically soundproof. From a tiny cool kit which the Spider always wore strapped beneath his left arm, Wentworth extracted a slender probe of surgical steel and the locks yielded swiftly to his lock-pick. It was a satisfaction to have his tools again.

The basement of the building was a large dining room and behind it was a kitchen, both deserted now. He made his way rapidly upward through halls that were dimly lighted. Shreds of faint illumination slitted out from under some of the doors. Behind one, a man was humming in a light, throaty voice. In another, a woman quarreled monotonously in a high, tedious tone. How was he to find Yvonne? He smiled slightly, mock-ingly.

It shouldn't be too difficult. She used a musky perfume which, for some unknown reason, underworld women seemed to prefer. That scent should penetrate half a dozen wooden doors. There was no trace of it here, and the Spider climbed to the next floor. The hall was chiefly redolent of stale cigarette smoke and he made the rounds of the doors, listening at each in turn, sniff-ing. It struck Wentworth as grimly humorous that he should be sniffing for a trail like a bloodhound. Queer that he felt so buoyant after his spell of depression. Even the fact that there were gangsters in the building who would rush to kill him at the slightest alarm did not bother him.

Well, the musk trail had failed him. He would have to try another method, simply walk into one of these rooms and force its occupant to tell where Yvonne was. Afterwards, a few knots would keep that person from broadcasting an alarm…. Went-worth's hand, thinly gloved now, went to a doorknob. He twisted it gently, thrust, and sprang into the room with gun drawn. Then he smiled, heeled the door shut. He was in a luxuriously sensu-ous bedroom, all pink taffeta drapes and over-cushioned divans. Luck had been with him….

Wentworth said, "Pff! What a stench, my dear Yvonne. Really, you should retain a better perfumer."

Yvonne Musette crouched like a cat in the middle of her over-draped bedroom. Her negligee was black and diaphanous, but her manner was the reverse of alluring.

"I can't understand," the Spider went on gently, "why the stench didn't penetrate to the hall…. Say, Yvonne, why did El Gaucho pull Tommy Barker to pieces with the horses?"

THE SUDDENNESS of his questions seemed to stun her. She straightened out of the crouch, her face white beneath the scarlet of her lips. A tremor raced over her.

"No, no!" she cried out. "He didn't do that! He wouldn't dare. I send word by Peterson that Barkaire is to be safe. I lofe him. If that Gauch' 'ave—" Her words closed her throat. Her eyes widened, staring into the Spider's harshly sinister face. *"Les chevaux! The 'orses! O Mon Dieu*, no!"

The Spider nodded his head slowly. "If it was not Barker, then whom did El Gaucho put to the horses?"

Yvonne shook her head. She lifted her hands to the side of her face and pushed them up into her hair, rocked her head between them. "No, no!" she whispered. "He could not do that to my Barkaire…. Why, Why… *le canaille! Fils d'une cochone!* I keel him!"

Wentworth studied the woman with his cold gray-blue eyes and he judged that, as much as she could, she loved Tommy Barker.

But how far would she be willing to go to save him? These French women of *les Apaches* knew no limit.

"Listen," he said. "When we were in the plane flying west, Barker tried to turn me loose and El Gaucho held him prisoner.

He has promised to tear him apart with the horses. I've got to find El Gaucho so I can turn Barker loose, see?"

Yvonne's eyes were blank with terror, but as Wentworth spoke, she grew calmer and moved toward him. Suspicion was in her glance now.

"Why you do that?" she asked swiftly. "Barkaire and you not friends. Barkaire is wit' Peterson's gang. For why?"

Wentworth looked steadily into the woman's eyes. "Barker means a great deal to me," he said.

She came even closer, her black eyes flicking back and forth as she searched his face. "What is the truth?" she asked swiftly. "You are hiding somethin'. He mean' a great deal to you. Why?"

"Why does a son mean a lot to his father?" he asked quietly.

Yvonne's eyes widened on his face, then abruptly she threw her arms about his neck. "You are his *father!* You!" She danced back from him, her black eyes sparkling. "He is… your son, but not your wife's son, eh? Oh, I know, I know! Oh, my Barkaire's father. That is nize. Soo nize!"

Wentworth cut her short with a sharp gesture. He had allowed her to infer precisely that because he could see no other way, short of torture, of forcing her to tell what she knew.

"You see," he said swiftly, "why I must find El Gaucho and Tommy. I've *got* to. Tell me now. Where is El Gaucho? What is he planning to do?"

Yvonne shrugged, searching Wentworth's face with her eyes. "He come to New Yor' sometime tonight. He send 'is plan' to theese 'ouse and many men downstair' get them ready to mail to all othaire men. What they 'ave to do and w'en? Theese Gauch' one, he do many funny things!"

The Spider's eyes brightened with triumph, but he looked down at the platinum cigarette case he had slipped from his vest pocket lest the expression show. He offered Yvonne a cigarette, holding the case so that she must take one of three at the left hand side of the container. Then he took one from the other section and lighted both.

"El Gaucho comes to this building?"

Yvonne shrugged. "I do not know w'ere 'e come," she said. "Listen, you do not objec' to Barkaire and me? He is so nize boy. I teach 'im much. Please?"

WENTWORTH SHRUGGED. "I have very little control over Tommy," he said truthfully. "He will probably do just what he chooses." He was watching her secretly and saw her drag the back of her hand upward across her forehead, pushing up her black hair. He crushed out his own cigarette and stepped toward her, caught her under the arms and carried her to the bed. She protested weakly, but the fumes of the cigarette which Wentworth had given her were fuddling her brain. A moment after the Spider laid her down, she had fallen into a deep narcotic sleep.

Wentworth locked the door, pocketed the key. Then he slipped down the steps, bearing the blade of his sword-cane as he went. The heavy thorn-wood of the stick was clenched like a club in his left hand, the abbreviated rapier, ready in his right. These buildings were nearly soundproof, but a forty-five caliber bullet made a terrific racket between walls....

Swiftly, he made his way to the room that Yvonne had indicated, stooped to peer through the keyhole. There were only two men there, leaning back smoking cigarettes beside a great pile of sealed envelopes. It was apparent that their work was done, for a gray-striped mail bag lay beside them. The Spider turned the knob carelessly and strode in. One man stared wide-mouthed and startled into the grim Spider's face. The other fumbled as he snatched for his gun. He opened his mouth to shout a warning and, almost instinctively, the Spider's rapier speared into the opening. The man's cry was instantly dead as the blade slipped through his tongue and death came a moment later.

The second man was recovering now from his fright, but his gun accomplished no more. He tried to drop behind the table, but the sword blade found his throat and dropped him there a moment, with his chin against the steel, until Wentworth withdrew it. There was a fierce scowl upon the Spider's face and he stooped once beside each man, pressing to their foreheads the base of his cigarette lighter. When he had risen again, his seal glowed like a vermilion threat upon each brow.

With swift hands, Wentworth thrust the sealed envelopes into the gray mail bag and, three minutes after his entrance, Wentworth was creeping downward to the basement exit. He had to thrust his rapier through another man in the darkness of the basement hallway, but there was no further interruption to his retreat. The Daimler glided from the shadows and, a half-hour later, he was back in his own penthouse, fifteen stories above the street. On the way home, he had skimmed through a dozen of the letters.

They were not, as he had expected, exclusively directions for New York. They envisaged, too, the *destruction by bombs of eleven major cities of the United States!*

CHAPTER 15
BATTLE LINES

WITH HORROR dawning in his eyes, as Wentworth realized the incredible scope of El Gaucho's intended assault upon America, he turned toward Nita, who had come to his penthouse to await his return after she had performed the errand he had assigned her. Nita came swiftly toward him.

"You must rest, beloved," she said warmly. "You are weary. When did you sleep?"

Wentworth swept aside her words with a sharp gesture of his arm. "No, no," he cried. "There is no time to be lost. It's gigantic, this thing. We have never had anything like this. Never in all my battles with the Underworld has such a fiend arisen. Why, damn it, Nita, he's going to destroy a dozen cities! Think of the thousands who will die...."

Nita's arms went about Wentworth's shoulders. "Dick, in justice to your cause, you must rest. Commissioner Flynn isn't convinced. He says he'll come around in the morning and see your proofs."

Wentworth tossed the gray mail bag to the table and stood looking at it. No one ever believed in danger until the criminals were at their very doors, until they had swept the forces of law and order from the field and were marauding among the innocent sheep…. Even the Commissioner of Police doubted. Wentworth's wide, confident shoulders sagged a little. He realized, suddenly, that his sleep had been a broken nap in a plane and that his food had been not of the best… and that there were many hours of strenuous battle ahead. Damn it, they could not wait until morning. The attack was four days from now, but four days was a pitifully short time for preparation when there were traitors in all strongholds….

"Flynn must come here tonight," Wentworth said savagely. "There is no time to wait! Isn't Kirkpatrick in town? I glimpsed a headline in a paper…."

Nita's violet eyes held him. Her voice was low, warm. "Steady, dear," she said. "I doubt that you will have much rest from now on, Dick. And… you are strained. Everything depends on you. Give me an hour, Dick, to rest you. I will call Flynn and Kirkpatrick and ask them to come in an hour."

Wentworth hesitated, aware of the exhaustion of all his faculties. He knew the wisdom of what Nita said. It was not his habit to drive himself too far, for he knew exactly how long he could continue to force weary mind and body along. After all, it was only an hour. He said, "You are right, Nita. By all means, call Flynn and Kirk."

Jenkyns brought them food after Nita had made her call, and they sat together on a deep divan and drank strong coffee laced with cognac, ate delicate pigeon's eggs, beaten up with sugar and hot sherry. Then Nita bade the Spider rest. She slid her soft arm beneath his head, pressed her lips to his forehead and cheeks, to his tired eyes. Her white hand smoothed away the ache from his forehead.

Supine, relaxing from the inner muscles outward and breathing more and more deeply, as the *yogis* had taught him in ancient Lahore, the Spider rested, absorbing love, purity, unselfishness and faith from the radiant girl who poured it out to him. So he prepared himself for battle. Strength seemed actually to flow from Nita to Wentworth. Finally, she relaxed there by him on the divan and the two slept.

IT WAS there Jenkyns' wise old eyes found them later when Flynn and Kirkpatrick came together to the aerie of the Spider, far above Fifth Avenue. For a full minute, the butler who had served Wentworth's father before him stood there looking, sadness on his ruddy, wrinkled face. His eyes misted. He would not have known how to say what he felt: that it was a pity for such bright beauty and such virile, superb youth, to be always dancing in a duel with death.

Jenkyns cleared his throat politely and they were both instantly, awake, sat smiling up at him.

"Ask them if they will wait ten minutes," Nita said when he spoke. "Master Dick is resting."

She led Wentworth to the terrace, where they stood together in the moonlight and looked down on the city. The sight braced them, sent every trace of languor from them. Wentworth knew, as he looked, that he never had loved this city more, the bright jewel of the Western world, and he had never loved the vast reaches of the country as well; this fair land that El Gaucho sought to destroy. Commissioner Flynn and Governor Kirkpatrick felt almost an electric shock of vitality when they came into the presence of the two.

Commissioner Patrick O. Flynn had been a brigadier general in the army and the military imprint was strong upon his lean, angular body. Even the iron-gray hair on his narrow head seemed still to bear the imprint of his officer's cap.

"The proof?" he asked, laconic as always. It was his greeting.

Wentworth gestured toward the mail bag. "There's the tangible evidence," he said, his voice crisp and full. "I'll tell you about it presently."

He turned toward Governor Kirkpatrick, who was waiting to one side with a deep smile on his saturnine face. While Flynn turned to the evidence, Wentworth strode toward Kirkpatrick and their hands clasped strongly, the keen gray-blue eyes of the Spider looked into blue eyes that could be as frosty as his own.

"It's been a long time since I saw you," Kirkpatrick said gravely. "Damn your eyes, where have you been keeping yourself? I believe you got me elected to the governorship just so you could get me out of the way."

Wentworth laughed, saying nothing, throwing an arm about the hard shoulders of the Governor. They were not demonstrative, these two men, but they were old friends, dating from the days when Kirkpatrick had been Commissioner of Police and Wentworth had been his hated enemy, the Spider. Not that Wentworth ever admitted in so many words to Kirkpatrick that he was the Spider.... There was no need. Kirkpatrick had been sure and had directly told Wentworth so, but he had added that he admired this stern wolf of justice who called himself the

Spider; that so long as no positive evidence fell into his hands, he would assist Wentworth; but if that proof ever came to his attention, he would prosecute to the best of his ability.

The understanding remained between them that way. Kirkpatrick had refused once to pardon Wentworth when he was sentenced to die on what was proved afterward to be a framed murder charge. And Wentworth had not appealed to him to help. These two understood each other and each respected the other for the man that he was.

Even this after-midnight call had not caught Kirkpatrick carelessly attired. He was faultless in evening dress, a gardenia gracing his lapel, his black hair smooth and ordered on his scalp. The points of his militant, black mustache were carefully waxed. Wentworth took in these outward aspects of his friend's well-being in a glance and was glad, for travail lay ahead for him, too.

FLYNN LOOKED up at the two from where he stood beside the letter-littered table. "Monstrous!" he said sharply. "Monstrous! All details of plot, Kirkpatrick. Every damned one. Eleven cities."

"I can tell you more briefly than you can dig it from that mass of detail," Wentworth said, his voice harshening. "Here's a summary:

"Number one. Instructions to the Graling gang in Boston. All harbor shipping and piers except those containing very valuable cargo to be blown up at midnight. All police stations and headquarters ditto. Bridge over the Charles, same. El Gaucho is sending armed forces to supplement the gangsters and they are to be placed with an incredibly keen eye for strategy. "Number two, San Francisco. First of all, a break on Alcatraz Island, releasing all prisoners...."

"Can't be done," snapped Flynn. "Good God! Powerful prison. One of the strongest...."

"Not even with keepers in the plot?" Wentworth asked softly.

"Good God!" gasped Flynn.

"This thing has been going on for years," Wentworth explained. "Ever since this Gaucho and Von Hapszollern and De Moltkez got together and aggravated one another's egos until they became monsters. I tell you, this is an octopus which will strangle us with a thousand arms unless we understand what we are fighting.

"Well, San Francisco. All police stations and Headquarters, all officers *and* homes of officials of law and order, and all shipping which can be a means of defense, are to go up at the same moment that the same is happening in Boston.

"Every large city in this country *and* in Canada is to receive the same treatment, simultaneously. They are going to prevent our neighbor and friend from coming to our aid by destroying Canada; I tell you El Gaucho already regards the United States, Canada, Mexico and Central and South America as his kingdom!

"Mark that the police headquarters and stations and shipping of New York are to be spared 'if possible.' And why? Because this is to be Gaucho's capital. He regards its building and shipping with a fond eye. He intends to reduce all other cities to much less than their present size and importance. He plans to extend

New York clear down to the end of Long Island and there to have the gigantic harbor that we, ourselves, ought to have started twenty years ago.

"As for our soldiers, the third who are already El Gaucho's men—oh, yes, Flynn, it's true—will by various pretexts draw away from the main body on the appointed night and touch off the mines, long since laid, which will blow every soul to bits. West Point is to be gassed along with Annapolis." Wentworth paused, looking at the two men before him. His own breathing had quickened.

Kirkpatrick said gravely, "It's the worst yet, Dick."

WENTWORTH NODDED. "The worst ever fought. It's damnable. Even in Washington there's treachery, especially among many of the foreign legations. You must remember that Bethania and Ruthia are regarded with almost superstitious awe by Europe. They have unbroken lines of kings, running back to Roman days. This Gaucho and Von Hapszollern are the real thing, so far as that goes—rotten, if a plain American's opinion holds—with about one thousand too many years of believing themselves God's anointed rulers over the rest of the world.

"Here are the plans that were to go to every chief city tonight. I don't know that it was tonight, but I am sure that their duplicates with some details changed, must go, if the great night is to come off. We have *just four days* in which to meet this catastrophe—just four days to organize a decent democratic existence, not only for ourselves, Flynn, Kirk, not only for our country, but for the entire world!"

"This man, with his ability to half-hypnotize men… the same thing that made Napoleon a menace, that made

Hitler a menace—this man has in even greater degree, and, what is more, he has the terrible fascination which utter cruelty has. If you had seen—"

Wentworth stopped abruptly. He could not admit his identity as the Spider. "If you had seen something which he did recently, how he enjoyed the sight of the most dreadful human suffering and how steadily and calmly he contemplated what drove the most hardened men almost mad to witness—and if you had seen how that very ability of his hypnotized those hard men—you'd know what I mean."

The Commissioner and Governor Kirkpatrick, faces very white, looked at Wentworth for a long moment.

"You are right," Kirkpatrick said tightly. "By God! What it would have meant if you had not discovered all this!"

The governor strode forward, clasped his hand. "Dick, boy, you're a wonder. But what in heaven's name are we going to do?"

Wentworth said gravely, "We can take every possible precaution against him. We can guard the points he has listed to destroy. Regardless of the fact that we have his plans, any attack he makes must envisage destruction of the same places."

Nita had listened gravely. Now she stepped forward. She had never been more beautiful, Wentworth thought, her whole body radiating her woman's indomitable spirit.

"Listen," she said, "make this a headquarters for the battle. For it will be a battle, you know, from the first. There are traitors and treachery everywhere. Police headquarters, any place you used, would be full of spies. But this place, we can protect and defend. Let me have a dozen women stenographers and typists. Women are less apt to have been bought in by El Gaucho, since his every action indicates his contempt of the sex, his oversight of our possibilities. Put in radio equipment, a half-dozen trunk-lines and a telephone switchboard...."

Kirkpatrick frowned down at the floor, his hand going slowly to his mustache as always when he was puzzled or worried. Gravely, he nodded.

"It's a good plan, Flynn."

Flynn looked about the room sharply and Wentworth's lifted hand brought Jenkyns with a telephone which he plugged in near the Commissioner. He got police headquarters and Flynn's brisk, military voice began to bark orders. Wentworth turned to Nita, pressed his lips to her check, then his hand clasped hers in a firm, steady, comrade's grip. That, they both knew, was the last time that either could think of the other except as a human pawn in the battle for the life of the country, neither to be considered again in the face of the world's safety.

AS HE turned toward the door, a tall figure in spotless white entered the room and bowed smoothly, touching cupped hands to his brow.

"*Salaam, sahib!*" he murmured.

Wentworth caught Ram Singh by the shoulders, gripping hard. "My heart is made glad," he said in swift Hindustani, "to find you strong and well again. It has come to my ears how you fought for me and for the *missie sahib*, and I give you honor, Ram Singh. Verily, thou art a great warrior!"

Ram Singh's white teeth flashed in a smile. *"Wah! Sahib!* It was nothing. Those were not men, but mice who scampered at the sight of a warrior's knife!"

Wentworth smiled. "Ram Singh," he said, growing grave, "I have a task for thee."

"Han, sahib!"

"A great battle is ahead. This, my home, will be the heart of that battle," he said, "and my heart, too, will be here."

Ram Singh's eyes flashed to Nita, standing just behind his master's shoulder.

"Yes," said Wentworth, "thou art my strong warrior. With you here, my heart will be safe. My courage will be strong. Guard, Ram Singh."

"Han, sahib!" Ram Singh's assent rang like a trumpet. He stepped back, shoulders against the wall, arms folded across his deep chest, and Wentworth knew that he would die with many wounds before he would permit harm to come to Nita.

Governor Kirkpatrick looked on with keen, intelligent eyes. "I take it you won't be with us, Dick?" he commented quietly.

Wentworth turned toward him. "I'm going to seek out El Gaucho himself," he said. "He will be destroyed in battle and as long as he lives, with the magic of his personality, he can continue to generate new armies against humanity. As for staying here, there is no need of me. You can do what must be done as well—better than I!"

"Not better, Dick," Kirkpatrick said, "but we will do our best. Do you know where to go for this El Gaucho?"

"Only a clue," Wentworth said grimly. "A weak clue, but it

must lead to success. I have also a plan which is based on the fact that El Gaucho has offered to pay its weight in gold to the man who brings him the Spider's head. You can see how serious it is.

"It is not Europe against America. It is an arch-fiend—a madman—against all the rest of the world. We cannot, we *shall* not fail!"

CHAPTER 16
A GRIM TASK

WENTWORTH DID not at once leave the apartment. He retired to his bedroom and went swiftly to work with makeup kit. He altered his mouth so that it had a one-sided sneer, and his eyes, too, participated in the leer, drooping at their outer corners. Cleverly placed bits of wax in his nostrils flattened out the bridge and gave him a heavy, noisy habit of breathing. He parted his hair in the middle and let strands straggle on his forehead. He was not a prepossessing creature and the clothing he donned did not help.

Afterward, he worked for an hour in his laboratory and when he came out, he carried a black satchel which bulged about some rounded object. He slipped back then to the drawing room and showed himself suddenly in a doorway. Kirkpatrick started to his feet, hand flipping to a gun beneath his armpit, and Ram Singh's knife flashed to his hand. Wentworth lifted his arms.

"Gosh sake, guv'nor," he whined, "give a guy a chance!"

Nita laughed. "For heaven's sake, Kirk," she said, "haven't you got used to Dick's tricks yet?"

"Dick!" Kirkpatrick holstered his gun. "Damn your soul, Dick, you had me scared for a minute!"

Flynn regarded him grimly. "You're good at that stuff," he grunted. "Wish I had a few of you in the department."

Nita's laughter was soft. "There's only one Dick Wentworth, Commissioner!"

Wentworth bowed with his customary suavity. "I am more than flattered," he said. "Well, I'm off. Look for me… when you see me."

Kirkpatrick smiled wryly. "And we probably won't know you when we do!"

They were all laughing when he left, but Wentworth's own face was grim beneath its disguise and there was a hard bitterness in his soul. It was necessary that they should have confidence, these friends and allies of his, but only Wentworth knew how titanic was the struggle ahead. Even before he had left, Kirkpatrick had been having trouble getting telephonic messages through to warn distant cities of El Gaucho's plot. Telegraph companies reported "indefinite delays."

On the second floor of the apartment building, Wentworth left the elevator and went to a front window in spite of the protest of the operator, who did not like his looks. At the window Wentworth drew a monocle from his vest pocket and squinted through it at the top of a new Ford coupé parked at the curb. He nodded in satisfaction, returned to the elevator and its glowering operator.

Once in the Ford he had inspected, Wentworth sped northward along Fifth Avenue. His Hispano-Suiza roadster would have been more to his liking, but this car was fast enough for all practical purposes and it was inconspicuous—more suited to the character he had assumed.

The Spider made good time through the almost deserted streets. It was nearly three o'clock in the morning and there was nothing moving except a few nighthawk taxis and skylarking private cars. All of which was perfectly suited to Wentworth's purposes. He was speeding to the home of a high police official whose name had been on the payrolls of El Gaucho, a man whose record was studded with brutal actions, but who had retained his position because of political influence which transcended even that of Commissioner Flynn.

He had been one of those the Spider had marked down for his vengeance before the uprising of El Gaucho had swept all minor criminalities from consideration....

DELIBERATELY, WENTWORTH had secreted the letter addressed to that man. He was for private vengeance—and it was possible the man's death might yet serve the people he had betrayed. Wentworth's hand, as he thought of this, went to a stout walking cane beside him, a cane which covered a straight, two-edged sword. Even his wrist, made more sinister by the details of the disguise he had assumed, was a fearful thing. It was a fearful thing that he planned to do, but the end—which would be the death of El Gaucho—was full justification to his Spider's mind, however much Richard Wentworth might shrink from the deed ahead.

Forty minutes after leaving his apartment, Wentworth parked his car beside a rather elaborate estate in Pelham Manor, an exclusive suburb on Long Island Sound. He caught up the cane, the black handbag and a rubberized blanket from beside him and stole toward the place. A husky dog rushed toward him, bellowing an alarm, and the stick swung once. Thereafter, deep silence lay upon the place. Wentworth crouched motionless in the shadow of a shrub for ten minutes before he was confident no one had been awakened. Then he stole forward again.

Wentworth, creeping upon the home of Lieutenant Schwartz, was as silent as the death he came to bring. A basement window yielded to a glass cutter, Wentworth removing the excised segment with a suction cup that he attached to its surface. Five dragging minutes later, he was on the second floor of the house.

There were three men in the house, no women. Wentworth pricked the throat of two of these men with a narcotic needle that deepened their sleep, then he stole to the master bedroom, where Lieutenant Schwartz slept between silken sheets. Wentworth's lips drew back from his teeth at sight of the sensually luxurious room. Where would an honest lieutenant of police obtain the money for such quarters?

Wentworth flicked on the lights of the room, drew his sword from its wooden case with a thin whisper of fine steel and walked toward the bed. The man who slept there was brawnily built, but lines of dissipation marked his face. Well, those could easily be changed....

Lieutenant Schwartz awoke with a jerk of muscles, a leap that carried him three feet from the side of his bed, revolver in hand. He leveled it at the Spider, staring in amazement at the man before him with the short, heavy-bladed sword in his hand.

But his surprise passed and a slow, thick-lipped smile crossed his face.

"Well, well," he drawled, "what the hell do you think you're doing here?"

Wentworth smiled, hard-eyed. "I have come to kill you, Lieutenant Schwartz. In fact, I have come to cut off your head!"

Schwartz's revolver trembled a little in his hand. The sleep flush faded from his cheeks and he retreated a quick, frightened step. Something in the supremely confident manner of the Spider—his conversational statement of a terrifying fact—utterly disconcerted the man. He knew as he retreated that here was no ordinary criminal invading a rich house to rob. His bulging eyes shifted before the steady gaze of Wentworth.

"Who... *Who are you?*" he whispered.

Wentworth laughed and the sound was flat and mocking, sinister as night. It was a sound that many a criminal had heard before his death, this laughter of the Spider. And others had heard it, too, and trembled at its mere memory.

"You asked," Wentworth purred softly, "who I am. Well, I'll tell you... I am... *the Spider!*"

A TERRIFIED shriek rose from Schwartz's throat, for as Wentworth pronounced *the Spider* he sprang forward with his sword sweeping upward, then forward in a resistless slash. He did not spring blindly onto the muzzle of the gun. He saw Schwartz thrust the weapon forward in his terror, jerking at the trigger. It was no trick for a man with the split-second reflexes of the Spider to knock that weapon's muzzle aside with a swift blow of the cane's scabbard. His sword swung true, its thin steel edge hissing a little song of death…. There was no second shot.

Afterward, the rubberized blanket a heavy burden on his shoulder, Wentworth made his swift, silent way to his car and deposited what he carried in the rumble seat. His black bag he set upon the seat beside him. His face was down and there was a haggard darkness about his eyes. An hour and twenty minutes after he left his apartment, Wentworth tooled the car again into the northernmost end of Fifth Avenue. He slowed then, drifted southward, watching the thin scattering of traffic. Finally, in the Twenties, he swerved to the curb. Only one taxi was in sight and that turned a corner and vanished as he parked. He flipped open the rumble seat and dragged out the rubberized blanket.

The headless body which he laid upon the sidewalk bore no resemblance to that of the pajamaed man he had killed. There was a long black cape from its shoulders, and on the pavement beside it, Wentworth tossed a broad-brimmed black hat such as the Spider wore.

Wentworth sprang to the car again and raced to a nearby all-night drug store, sidled into a booth and called police head-quarters excitedly.

"Geez!" he gasped into the mouthpiece. "I just saw the Spider and another guy fighting up on Fifth Avenue—Twenty-seventh, I t'ink it was. Sure! Yeah! Listen, if you catch him do I get the reward, huh?"

He heard the cop's voice grow excited, too, and then he hung up and slipped from the booth, got his car away fast. He was in the crowd that assembled a few minutes later when police radio-cars raced to the spot and found the headless body on the sidewalk.

Wentworth nudged the man next to him in the crowd. "Geez!" he whispered. "It's the Spider! See that there cape? See the hat? It's the Spider!" His whisper raced through the crowd, such a group of men as will assemble any hour of the day or night in New York, seemingly appearing almost from the sidewalks when there is something to excite their morbid curiosity. The police growled out the words, too, the magical words that could strike terror to a thousand hearts: *"The Spider!"*

Wentworth's work was accomplished for the night, but he did not return to the penthouse where the forces of the law were mobilizing their strength. He went to a hotel. He insisted on carrying the black bag which bulged so oddly in the middle to his room. Once there, he threw himself down for the sleep he had been needing. The Spider could sleep for a while now. Kirkpatrick would do everything that was possible, and the campaign of the Spider must wait for a few hours, wait until the newspapers screamed aloud that the Spider was dead, his head hacked from his shoulders and his body left on the pavements on Fifth Avenue.

CHAPTER 17
CELL FOR THE SPIDER

FIVE HOURS' sleep sufficed Wentworth and he awoke greatly refreshed, spent a luxurious twenty minutes bathing, then resumed his shoddy identity and sent out for the morning newspapers. The discovery of the false Spider's body had been late for even the final edition, but all of the dailies had made over the front page with heavy eight-column headlines screaming that the Spider was dead. Even the cautious *Times* seemed reasonably certain of the dead man's identity. From somewhere, too, had come information that El Gaucho had offered to redeem the head of the Spider with its weight in gold....

His restless necessity for action drove Wentworth from his hotel room though he had intended to remain idle most of the day, gathering his resources, husbanding his strength for the crucial battle—more critical than ever—which loomed for him. With the black handbag, over whose contents he worked before he left, he spent the day in the usual criminal haunts of the city. Police patrols of four kept watch in the district, but did nothing to prevent the harsh whispers that were heard everywhere.

"El Gaucho is coming! He'll be king!"

But no one seemed to know where El Gaucho was, or when he would come, or what he would do next. Wentworth had a few addresses of Gaucho's allies which he had taken from the gang orders, but he did not wish to approach any one of the men named openly, lest suspicions be aroused. Finally, he was forced to that expedient.

He went to a hotel where one Arthur Morrow was supposed to be registered and bribed a bellhop to point the man out to him in the lobby. Afterward, he took a seat beside the man and hugged the black bag to his chest. Arthur Morrow was fat, with a face that seemed the genial wrinkled countenance of most fat men until the shifty, small greenish eyes were studied. After that, there could be no question of his true nature. In Wentworth's disguised face, his subtly furtive manner, Morrow recognized a kindred being. He wheezily offered Wentworth a cigarette. Wentworth curtly refused, moved a little away from Morrow. It was exactly the move calculated to arouse the criminal's interest. Morrow watched silently for awhile, then bent forward.

"Listen, pal," he whispered, "you don't need to be scared of me. I ain't no dick."

Wentworth eyed him suspiciously. There was shrewdness in this fat man, and danger, too.

"I don't give a damn what you are," Wentworth said roughly, and slid the black bag around on the opposite side of his body.

Morrow wheezed with laughter. "Cripes, you're a lousy crook," he said. "Anybody would know you had swag in that bag of yours."

"That's what you think!" Wentworth jeered.

Arthur Morrow heaved to his feet and towered over Wentworth's cringing body. There was greed in his beady little eyes, and he was bold with the expected glory to come, with the confidence the Underworld felt in El Gaucho.

"Listen, rat," snarled Morrow, "you're coming up to my room, see, and we're going to talk."

Wentworth slid out past his big body. He was defiant and cringing at once, in the manner of petty crooks. "Geez, I ain't done nothin'," he whined. "I was just sittin' here and you have to pull this stuff. There ain't nothin' in the bag except some clothes...."

"Upstairs," Morrow grunted. He leaned forward, pushing his fat face close to Wentworth's. "Listen, crook. Did you ever hear of El Gaucho?"

Wentworth's face lighted with eagerness. "Say, do you know him? Say, where's your room?"

IN THE elevator going upward, Wentworth leaned close to the fat man. "Listen," he said. "You get me to the Gaucho and I'll split with you. This here bag is worth its weight in gold to Gaucho."

Arthur Morrow's little eyes squeezed almost shut. *"Its weight in gold!"* he said softly. He looked furtively at Wentworth and when they went along the hallway toward his room, they walked side by side, each watching the other. They went into the room with locked gaze.

Morrow locked the door, came close to Wentworth. "Listen," he said. "What you said has got me interested as all hell. There ain't but one thing worth its weight in gold to El Gaucho. Just one, and you...." He stared deeply into Wentworth's eyes and stepped back a quick step, hand fluttering toward his coat pocket. He didn't draw a gun, but he kept his fat hand close to his pocket while he studied the leering face of Wentworth's disguise.

Wentworth laughed, set the bag down on the bed with a little swagger.

"What's in the bag?" Morrow whispered.

Wentworth laughed. "You wouldn't want to see," he jeered. Seemingly, he had gained confidence from the other's manner. He chuckled when Morrow licked his over-red lips. "No, you

The Spider's head struck El Gaucho and he toppled to the ground!

wouldn't want to see what I got in that little black bag." He patted the hard bulge.

Morrow's eyes were wide now. "If you've got… what I think you've got," he wheezed. "I'll… By God, I'll take you to El Gaucho himself!" He took a step nearer, licking his lips. "Let's see!"

Wentworth appeared to consider for a moment, then he opened the bag, stepped back with a wave of his hand. He slid a hand to his coat lapel then, with Morrow's eyes upon him.

"Go ahead and look," he said.

Morrow gingerly pulled open the sides of the bag, peered in and staggered back with his fat hands trembling. He swallowed with enormous effort.

"Cripes!" he whispered. "Cripes! How did you do it?"

Wentworth pulled his lips back from discolored teeth. "That's my business," he said thinly. "Gaucho promised to pay and I'm going to collect."

Morrow's eyes had turned crafty and the sneer on Wentworth's disguised face widened. His gun slipped smoothly into his palm.

"Listen, fat boy," he said, "I've promised you a cut if you'll take me to El Gaucho. But don't think you're going to get more than a cut. I killed the Spider and I guess I can take care of a fat skunk…."

"Don't call me fat!" Morrow spluttered, but he looked cowed. "Come on, get your bag and I'll take you…."

"We'll wait until dark," Wentworth snapped. "Cops can see too well now. I got a car and when it's night, we'll get in that and go for a ride, see? And if there's any funny business, you ain't comin' back from that ride."

Morrow snarled at him. "Listen, just because you killed the Spider...."

Wentworth pushed Morrow suddenly, tripped him on the bed and held him with a gun while he put cords he took from his pocket about the gangster's arms and legs.

Morrow lay breathing hard, hatred and cupidity quarreling in his eyes. "Listen, pal," he whined, "you hadn't ought to treat me this way. And listen, we can't wait till dark. It's a long trip up to where El Gaucho is and he's going to take this town at midnight. Hell, he'd... he'd kill me if I wasn't on the job then."

WENTWORTH'S HEART sprang painfully into his throat at the news. El Gaucho must have performed miracles to have his men ready to strike three days before the date set in the orders he was sending out. He would catch New York absolutely unprepared. The nation would be practically at his mercy, unless... unless the Spider could get through!

He paced up and down the floor with bowed head, thinking frantically. He had counted on a night trip. The top of the Ford he was driving had been painted with a preparation that threw off infrared rays which were invisible to the human eye. Jackson was cruising over the city in a small semi-rigid dirigible they had chartered from the Goodyear people and, by means of specially treated lenses, Jackson could spot the car with its infrared paint among a stream of other automobiles. Jackson was to follow him when he started for the headquarters of El Gaucho, then summon help by radio from the dirigible.

The infrared rays would be easily detected at night, but what would be the result by daylight? Wentworth could not know—yet he did not feel that he could afford to wait until darkness to make the attempt upon El Gaucho. Too much depended upon his success and there would be no margin of safety....

From the bed, Morrow pleaded, "Cripes, pal, you're puttin' me on the spot doin' this. Come on, let's go now."

Wentworth came to an abrupt decision.

"Okay, fats," the Spider snarled. "We'll go now, but if you try any double-cross on me, you fat louse, I'll shoot you to pieces, see?"

Morrow wheezed, "I see, pal. I wouldn't do nothin' like that."

"Of course not! Pal!" Wentworth freed Morrow from the bed after relieving him of two light guns he carried in his pockets. Then they went from the hotel, striding close together, Wentworth with the black bag in one hand, his gun in the other, though hidden in his pocket.

Morrow climbed into his car without protest and Wentworth, circling the coupé, had time to give a boy a telegram to Nita, which he had secretly written to warn her of El Gaucho's changed plans. He had time to glance upward and see that a dirigible was passing low and sluggishly over the street. He felt a thrill of hope.

Perhaps Jackson could actually detect infrared rays by daylight! His hope died almost as soon as it was born, for the dirigible passed on out of sight. Just cruising, apparently. With some forlorn idea of helping Jackson identify the car, he threw his cap upside down into the rumble seat. The cap had a red lining.

WENTWORTH CLIMBED in and began to drive by Morrow's directions. The black bag was beneath Wentworth's knees and he caught the fat man staring at it time after time, half in fascination, half in greed. The course lay northward toward Albany, and when Wentworth learned that he had a hundred and fifty miles to drive he began to bear down upon the accelerator. The light car lifted and bucked against the steering wheel. He longed for the smooth power of his Hispano or his Daimler, but neither could have served him in this day's crisis….

The sun was near the horizon when Morrow directed Wentworth to turn off the main road into a narrow dirt lane that zigzagged between the thick trunks of trees, dived sharply to ford a stream or surged upward over rocky slopes. When they had gone a mile along that road, a sentry challenged, his bayoneted rifle leveled at Wentworth's chest.

Morrow spoke eagerly to him. "This guy has got the Spider's head. We want to take it to His Majesty."

The sentry stepped back behind a tree and Wentworth perceived with narrowed eyes that there was a telephone there. The man talked for a swift minute, then waited for what seemed interminable hours while the car's engine chugged quietly and nothing moved about them at all. Finally the sentry came back.

"Morrow is to wait here. You go ahead," he told Wentworth.

Wentworth nodded, smiling thinly at Morrow. The fat man protested, but climbed out promptly. It was clear that El Gaucho obtained instantaneous obedience even among the least of his servitors. Wentworth heard the sentry tell Morrow, "A car will take you back to the city. You will be fined half your bonus for leaving your post."

Wentworth's lips were twisted wryly. He remembered another man who had been treated less kindly for leaving his post. Evidently, El Gaucho was anxious to receive the proof of his enemy's death.

Three sentries passed him without challenge and it became apparent that word had gone ahead. El Gaucho had his camp superbly protected. Undoubtedly these telephone-equipped guards surround the place in all directions. The first evidence of an invading force would instantly alarm El Gaucho's entire army of killers....

Wentworth drove past five more sentries before his car was stopped at a high, barbed-wire fence. He left it then, was stripped of his two forty-five caliber automatics, but allowed to retain the black bag at which men stared curiously. Here, once more, was the orderly array of earth-colored tents. Houses, too, were painted so as to make them inconspicuous. Wentworth recalled the other encampment in that sunken plateau far to the west and surmised that here El Gaucho had fewer allies among the air pilots who would be supposed to watch out for his headquarters.

THERE WERE three barbed-wire fences and each was backed by entanglements of long-spined wire and by trenches. Wentworth's heart sank with each new indication of power. Even if authorities did locate this place, it would take them days to move up the troops and equipment to destroy it, and the encampment was strategically placed atop a hill, the highest promontory anywhere about. Damn it, no one would have believed that such a thing as this was possible; an armed and entrenched force in the heart of America, ready to sweep the authorities of law and order from power.

Wentworth realized abruptly that he was not being taken toward the main, large building, but toward a smaller structure with barred windows. He halted in his tracks and the bayonets of four soldiers ringed him in.

"Listen," he said. "I want to see El Gaucho! I can go to jail any day." He lifted the black bag. "El Gaucho wants to see this!"

The sentries' bayonets pressed closer. "You will await word from His Majesty," one announced flatly, and there could be no more argument against those bare, steel blades. Wentworth was thrust into a cell and the door clanged sullenly behind him.

CHAPTER 18
THE SPIDER'S HEAD

LONG HOURS dragged past while Wentworth paced slowly back and forth in his cell. Beyond the wall of solid metal that separated him from the next cubicle, he could hear some other man pacing, too. It occurred to him fleetingly that it might be Tommy Barker. But there could be no communication between them, no help one for the other. He was in disguise, probably watched....

As the black night wheeled on, Wentworth's anxiety mounted. He could not fail, now that he was this near his goal. He could not! He had come prepared for possible imprisonment. Inside of his strong, white teeth, fastened to his lower molars and curved against the inner surfaces of his teeth was a saw blade of such tempered hardness that it would slice through the toughest steel. Within an hour, if unobserved, he could hack through the bars of his window.

But that was only a last extremity. It was an expedient to save his life. And what he wanted now was the death of

El Gaucho. If he escaped from his cell, he would have to force his way through armed sentries to the throne. If El Gaucho finally relented and permitted him to bring his black bag into his presence, there would be no difficulty at all. Wentworth was convinced there would be no help from Jackson. He had watched the evening skies in vain for any trace of the dirigible in which his man was to have followed him. No, it must all come from within himself.

The Spider stood motionless at the window of his cell, staring into the blackness. He closed his eyes, breathing strength into his body with deep inhalations. He was watching the time with sharp eyes. If he were not released and taken to El Gaucho, by quarter of twelve, he would have to burst from his cell, and take chances with death to reach El Gaucho.

The hands of his watch dragged to eleven-thirty, to twenty-five minutes of twelve. In a dozen cities throughout the United States, Wentworth knew that gangsters were preparing to strike. They would destroy buildings and leaders of American life. They would, in one titanic blow, smash American institutions to the earth, bring back the reign of tyranny and selfish greed to the world.

"It shall not happen," Wentworth whispered to himself. "It shall not!"

Twenty minutes of twelve now. Wentworth crossed to his black bag, picked it up with deliberate hands. His mouth was tight, his lips cold and hard against his teeth. It was a desperate chance, but he must take it in five minutes more....

Minutes limped by. The Spider stood on braced feet before the door. There was a stirring now out there beyond the jail door, the clop of horses' hooves... Wentworth's blood turned cold. Horses' hooves in this enclosed camp could mean but one thing. Someone had been doomed to death by the torture of the horses! Had a sentry penetrated his disguise? Had he been sentenced to that death? Or was it for Tommy Barker, prisoner somewhere in camp, perhaps in the cell next to his?

Wentworth jerked his head angrily. He could not think of such things when the fate of Christian civilization hung in the balance. Tom Barker, the Spider... they were nothing in the scales of justice. Wentworth crossed deliberately to the iron cot against the wall, picked up the black bag and returned to the door. It lacked only one minute of quarter to twelve....

Even as Wentworth prepared to take his last desperate measure, he heard rhythmic footsteps and knew that soldiers were marching toward the tiny, barred prison. The detail halted outside the building and four men entered, unlocked Wentworth's door and escorted him outside. After him, came the man from the other cubicle. Wentworth dared a glance in his direction and his heart gave a leap at the glimpse of a browned face, brave despite the haggard hint of what was to come, in his blue eyes. The boy carried his head high, his shoulders thrown back.

"I hope you've been feeding the horses well," he joked at one of the soldiers. "They're going to lose their dinner over what happens to me."

WENTWORTH LONGED to clap the boy on the back, shake his hand for that brave display, but he must act out his character. He carried himself with cringing insolence, hugging the black bag against his chest as if that were his protection against all evils, and his guarantee of heaven. Tommy Barker looked at him contemptuously.

The Spider's mind raced on ahead of the slow march of the soldiers toward the main building, which they circled deliberately. There was a white blaze of lights behind it and Wentworth knew that it was there the torture was to take place. Tommy Barker, and those great kind horses driven to murder by El Gaucho.... His eyes quested ahead. Files of soldiers as before, but few of the motley mob of killers that had witnessed the last execution. They would be in the cities, leading the gangsters who, within minutes, would destroy thousands.

There on the opposite side of this square of soldiers, drowned in blazing white light, stood the throne of El Gaucho and upon it the author of the hell that brewed above America tonight. He stood there upon the raised dais, arrogance in the lift of his head, utter confidence in his bearing.

When Wentworth, carrying out his part, had dropped to his knees before the throne; when Tommy Barker had been forced down into the dirt, El Gaucho turned his smile upon the assembled soldiers. Wentworth looked up into his bearded face and hugged the black bag. Such a slim chance.... His eyes flicked to the faces about the throne. De Moltkez with his right hand in a sling, Von Hapszollern in his Death's-Head Hussar's shako. Two women were by the throne, Carollotta—pale and straight-mouthed with some emotion that he could not discern—and Yvonne Musette!

Wentworth perceived that El Gaucho was about to make a speech.

"My people!" his deep voice boomed across the square of soldiers. "Tonight is the night of our glory. Tonight we triumph over all enemies. Here before us, we have one who will pay tonight for his opposition, and the head of one who already has paid. The Spider and the Spider's slave...!"

He paused and an obedient cheer rose from the assembled men. Carollotta swayed on her feet. Yvonne's red lips parted in that slow, cruel smile that Wentworth had seen once before when she had planned his murder.

"Here behind our throne," El Gaucho went on, in an expansive mood, "are telegraph instruments connecting us with all America. We will send to our allies the news of our triumph here, and they will bring us the news of our triumphs over a dozen cities, over all America."

El Gaucho flung out his arm. "Bring the horses!"

A QUIVER raced over Wentworth. Carollotta, despite her obvious effort at control, lifted a hand to her mouth and sank teeth into her wrist. Tom Barker turned toward Wentworth.

"If there's any justice on earth," he said vehemently, "you'll die by the vilest torture known. I'll bet you stabbed the Spider in the back!"

Barker was wrenched to his feet and pulled backward toward where the four great horses stood. Wentworth's heart beat high in his throat. There was a dryness in his mouth.

Wentworth looked up toward the throne. "Hey, Gauch'," he called, "how about making the slave kiss the Spider's head?"

El Gaucho stared sternly, but there was a gleam in his eyes that showed the proposal met with his approval.

"Bring me the head," he said.

Wentworth got to his feet and held the black bag in his two hands as he went forward, a soldier on either side of him. El Gaucho lifted his hand and a soldier whispered in Wentworth's ear.

"Hold up the head!"

The Spider's lips set grimly as he reached into the black bag. The time was not yet. These two soldiers… He grasped coarse hair, pulled the black bag clear and lifted a human head high into the air before him. Carollotta's sobs burst through the gag of her wrist and Wentworth saw her sag against the throne, weeping. Yvonne laughed and laughed. And El Gaucho….

El Gaucho leaned forward with his elbow on his knee and stared into the features of the Spider which Wentworth had built over the German features of Lieutenant Schwartz. El Gaucho nodded.

"It should be a heavy head," he said crisply. "You will earn high reward in our kingdom."

Then El Gaucho's eyes lifted above Wentworth's head and an eager light sprang into his eyes. He stood up.

"Wait!" he called, "I myself will fasten the last rope to the traitor."

The soldiers thrust Wentworth aside and El Gaucho stepped down from his throne, stalked toward where Tommy Barker lay supine upon the ground among the four horses. It was, Wentworth saw suddenly, the moment for which he had waited. It was now or never!

Wentworth jerked the head back over his shoulders and hurled it violently at El Gaucho! Skull struck skull and El Gaucho pitched forward in the dust. For a full dozen heartbeats there was absolute silence, absolute quiet over the entire assembly of soldiers. A deep curse groaned from Wentworth's throat. There was a bomb inside that skull, placed there while nausea wrenched at his stomach at the thing he did, while the Spider goaded himself with thoughts of his duty to humanity that could be performed in no other way. And *the bomb had failed to explode!* Even while he cursed at his failure, Wentworth sprang upon De Moltkez. He ripped the man's sword from its sheath, dragged its flying point across the officer's throat as he whirled toward the body of El Gaucho.

HE LIFTED the sword high over his head and in that same moment, Carollotta screamed a warning. Wentworth whirled, was barely in time to dash aside the sword of Von Hapszollern, stabbing at his back. A half-dozen soldiers rushed forward to strike him down but Von Hapszollern's snarling voice rang out.

"Hold!" he cried, "I claim the right to kill this dog!"

Wentworth found that he held in his hand only a nickel-plated dress sword. It had a sharp point which had done for De Moltkez, but it was very short and light, and the greater war saber of Von Hapszollern beat upon its feeble strength violently. The two men circled, Wentworth guarding against the attack of the other, looking for his chance to stab through the other's defense.

In a quick side-glance, he saw that El Gaucho had staggered to his feet and was looking stupidly about. He saw the duel, saw Wentworth's apparent helplessness and laughed aloud.

"Don't kill him, my friend," El Gaucho called to Von Hapszollern. "Just run him through the belly. Afterward, the horses may have their pleasure with him."

Von Hapszollern shouted a deep assent and El Gaucho turned toward Tommy Barker, supine among the horses. He laughed again and there was a thin, wild note to his laughter. Wentworth was allowing himself to be forced backward toward the throne now. Behind that were the telegraph instruments. Even in the midst of his desperate battle for life, Wentworth was thinking more of his country, of the people he loved, than of his own life. There was an indomitable strength in his arm tonight, for he fought not alone for himself, but for all those countless thousands over the nation who would die if he did not conquer.

Now he had achieved what he wanted. One foot was on the steps of the throne, the other braced before him, and his light sword moved like a flicker of light in and out of the slashing attack of Von Hapszollern.

"Carollotta," he whispered, "Carollotta!"

He heard her gasped response beside him and a smile touched his lips. He might yet win. It was a desperate venture....

"Carollotta," he whispered. "If you love Tommy, get a revolver and *shoot the head of the Spider!*"

He heard her sobs crowding against her teeth. Then the sound faded away from him. He hoped she would obey. Von Hapszollern was raging at his inability to break through the guard of this man who had cringed before the throne. He slashed wildly, recklessly, and Wentworth's defense grew more cautious, tighter. His wrist did not move more than four inches against the most dangerous of the prince's cuts.

But time grew short. There were only seconds now between him and midnight. Two minutes perhaps, maybe three. Certainly no more than that. Glancing beyond Von Hapszollern, Wentworth saw El Gaucho belaboring the great Percherons with a cat- o'-nine-tails that he had caught from one of the torturers. The horses stood, shivering in every muscle, but did not move. Wentworth gritted his teeth together. Why didn't Carollotta hurry? El Gaucho must have gone completely mad. No man could control a Percheron with a whip. Only kindness would move the great horses, and this fool....

Carollotta's voice whispered in his ear. "I have the revolver," she murmured, "but I have never fired one in my life."

Wentworth thrust back his left hand, caught the gun and at the same instant lunged furiously through Von Hapszollern's anger-opened guard. The light dress sword struck the golden buckle that held the baldric of Von Hapszollern's sword, glanced off, ripped cloth and flesh, then found its sheath in the prince's body. The blade snapped off short.

Wentworth sprang to El Gaucho's throne, the revolver held at his hip.

"If any man moves," he shouted, "El Gaucho dies. Carollotta,"—a whisper now—"go cut Tommy loose with Von Hapszollern's sword."

HE SAW the swift movement of the girl while his eyes quested over the amphitheater. Not one of the soldiers moved to lift his gun, but there were men near him who held their bayonets ready. If he lost control for a moment… Wentworth's thoughts were desperate. If only Carollotta would hurry. He didn't want to kill Tommy Barker if he could help it, but if he must… He glanced at his watch. One minute of twelve. For God's sake, Carollotta, hurry, hurry!

El Gaucho was still slashing at the Percherons with the heavy whip, failing to stir them from their tracks. Carollotta circled to get at Barker from the opposite side. Wentworth cursed. *In heaven's name, Carollotta. Don't you know that thousands of lives depend on your speed? I cannot wait any longer. I dare not. Thousands of lives against that of one man whom we both love. Our love is nothing.…*

Wentworth lifted the revolver, a hand on the back of the throne. He must fire and leap from the dais in the same split second of time, find the telegraph instruments… He could hear their tinny clicking there and subconsciously he listened. They were asking for the signal!

Merciful God, they would not strike until they had the signal from El Gaucho! But an officer was slipping behind the throne. There were only seconds between the Spider and death; between thousands and their doom; between civilization and its destruction…!

The bright blade of the saber Carollotta held flashed high in the air and slashed down, once, twice and Tommy Barker was scrambling to his feet. The whip of El Gaucho swept down and Barker cried aloud and fell back, hands rising to his face. Carollotta had been struck also by one of those lead-ended lashes and reeled backward, unconscious.

El Gaucho dropped his whip, sprang to the ropes to lash them once more to the man he would destroy. Wentworth caught a glimpse of his face as he bent, and there was utter madness there—the insanity of an egotist thwarted in his moment of triumph. A cry rose in Wentworth's throat. He lifted the revolver and fired—at the "head of the Spider" that lay on the ground. In the same moment, he hurled himself violently backward from the dais. He had a final glance as he leaped, of Yvonne Musette running to help El Gaucho, of her feet flying past the head of the Spider.…

Then everything was blacked out in a cataclysm of wind and sound. The bullet had exploded the bomb within the skull. Wentworth, safe behind the throne, peered out and saw a great crater in the earth, saw that Yvonne had vanished and saw something else that pulled him erect with a shout pouring from his lungs. El Gaucho was struggling between two of the horses who were rearing with fright after the blast. His arms were stretched out rigidly to each side of him toward the horses, as if… as if he himself were caught in the torture he had planned for Tommy Barker...!

And suddenly Wentworth understood. In his final, furious effort to destroy Barker, he had himself become entangled in the ropes of the horses! Shrill cries rosed from El Gaucho's lips, shrill screams of extreme agony. One great, ton-heavy Percheron reared into the air, its entire weight thrown against the tortured joints of El Gaucho's arms. And at once, the Percheron was racing across the field toward the bomb-scattered ranks of soldiers, and El Gaucho was being dragged in the opposite direction by a second horse, dragged through the dust, screaming and screaming. Then he was free of that horse, too, and ran shrieking in circles. But he did not throw his arms to heaven. He did not have any arms....

Behind the throne, feverish eyes on the dying man who had so nearly become king of America, Wentworth was pounding out messages on the telegraph keys.

"El Gaucho is dead," he sent. "El Gaucho is dead. Disband your gangs or you will die, too. The Spider swears it! El Gaucho is dead...."

AND EVEN as he sent that message, El Gaucho was collapsing out there among the men he had befuddled with his talk of glory, was dying in the dust where he had dragged so many others. Carollotta, in the dust, too, cradled Tommy Barker's head in her lap....

The roar of an explosion blasted over the armed camp. It was followed instantly by another and another and between the rumble of bombs, Wentworth caught the swooping, diving roar of airplanes. He sprang to his feet, flinging his hands in the air. Jackson! Jackson had followed after all, followed the car and had brought the bombing planes of the government to destroy this hell-hole of El Gaucho.

Slowly, Wentworth calmed, seeing the soldiers flee. He smiled gently, looking at Carollotta and Tommy Barker, their arms tight about each other, and he stole through the shadows that fell with the extinction of the lights, while the bombs still fell out there on the barbed-wire entanglements—to the car that had brought destruction to the power of El Gaucho.

When the soldiers of freedom came, they found Tommy and Carollotta. They found dead men… but the Spider had vanished!

POPULAR HERO PULPS AVAILABLE NOW:

THE SPIDER
- ❏ #1: The Spider Strikes — $13.95
- ❏ #2: The Wheel of Death — $13.95
- ❏ #3: Wings of the Black Death — $13.95
- ❏ #4: City of Flaming Shadows — $13.95
- ❏ #5: Empire of Doom! — $13.95
- ❏ #6: Citadel of Hell — $13.95
- ❏ #7: The Serpent of Destruction — $13.95
- ❏ #8: The Mad Horde — $13.95
- ❏ #9: Satan's Death Blast — $13.95
- ❏ #10: The Corpse Cargo — $13.95
- ❏ #11: Prince of the Red Looters — $13.95
- ❏ #12: Reign of the Silver Terror — $13.95
- ❏ #13: Builders of the Dark Empire — $13.95
- ❏ #14: Death's Crimson Juggernaut — $13.95
- ❏ #15: The Red Death Rain — $13.95
- ❏ #16: The City Destroyer — $13.95
- ❏ #17: The Pain Emperor — $13.95
- ❏ #18: The Flame Master — $13.95
- ❏ #19: Slaves of the Crime Master — $13.95
- ❏ #20: Reign of the Death Fiddler — $13.95
- ❏ #21: Hordes of the Red Butcher — $13.95
- ❏ #22: Dragon Lord of the Underworld — $13.95
- ❏ #23: Master of the Death-Madness — $13.95
- ❏ **NEW:** #24: King of the Red Killers — $13.95

THE MYSTERIOUS WU FANG
- ❏ #1: The Case of the Six Coffins — $12.95
- ❏ #2: The Case of the Scarlet Feather — $12.95
- ❏ #3: The Case of the Yellow Mask — $12.95
- ❏ #4: The Case of the Suicide Tomb — $12.95
- ❏ #5: The Case of the Green Death — $12.95
- ❏ #6: The Case of the Black Lotus — $12.95
- ❏ #7: The Case of the Hidden Scourge — $12.95

G-8 AND HIS BATTLE ACES
- ❏ #1: The Bat Staffel — $13.95

CAPTAIN SATAN
- ❏ #1: The Mask of the Damned — $13.95
- ❏ #2: Parole for the Dead — $13.95
- ❏ #3: The Dead Man Express — $13.95
- ❏ #4: A Ghost Rides the Dawn — $13.95
- ❏ #5: The Ambassador From Hell — $13.95

CAPTAIN ZERO
- ❏ #1: City of Deadly Sleep — $13.95
- ❏ #2: The Mark of Zero! — $13.95
- ❏ **NEW:** #3: The Golden Murder Syndicate — $13.95

OPERATOR 5
- ❏ #1: The Masked Invasion — $13.95
- ❏ #2: The Invisible Empire — $13.95
- ❏ #3: The Yellow Scourge — $13.95
- ❏ #4: The Melting Death — $13.95
- ❏ #5: Cavern of the Damned — $13.95
- ❏ #6: Master of Broken Men — $13.95
- ❏ #7: Invasion of the Dark Legions — $13.95
- ❏ #8: The Green Death Mists — $13.95
- ❏ #9: Legions of Starvation — $13.95
- ❏ #10: The Red Invader — $13.95
- ❏ #11: The League of War-Monsters — $13.95
- ❏ **NEW:** #12: The Army of the Dead — $13.95

DUSTY AYRES AND HIS BATTLE BIRDS
- ❏ #1: Black Lightning! — $13.95
- ❏ #2: Crimson Doom — $13.95
- ❏ #3: The Purple Tornado — $13.95
- ❏ #4: The Screaming Eye — $13.95
- ❏ #5: The Green Thunderbolt — $13.95
- ❏ #6: The Red Destroyer — $13.95
- ❏ #7: The White Death — $13.95
- ❏ #8: The Black Avenger — $13.95
- ❏ #9: The Silver Typhoon — $13.95
- ❏ #10: The Troposphere F-S — $13.95
- ❏ #11: The Blue Cyclone — $13.95
- ❏ #12: The Tesla Raiders — $13.95

DR. YEN SIN
- ❏ #1: Mystery of the Dragon's Shadow — $12.95
- ❏ #2: Mystery of the Golden Skull — $12.95
- ❏ #3: Mystery of the Singing Mummies — $12.95

MAVERICKS
- ❏ #1: Five Against the Law — $12.95
- ❏ #2: Mesquite Manhunters — $12.95
- ❏ #3: Bait for the Lobo Pack — $12.95
- ❏ #4: Doc Grimson's Outlaw Posse — $12.95
- ❏ #5: Charlie Parr's Gunsmoke Cure — $12.95

www.ingramcontent.com/pod-product-compliance
Lightning Source LLC
Chambersburg PA
CBHW020407180626
46812CB00003B/877